BROKEN DESTINY

THIEF OF HEARTS BOOK 3

C.R. JANE

MILA YOUNG

CONTENTS

Broken Destiny by C. R. Jane and Mila Young

Copyright © 2020 by C. R. Jane and Mila Young

All rights reserved.

No portion of this book may be reproduced in any form or by any electronic or mechanical means, including information storage and retrieval systems, without written permission from the author, except for the use of brief quotations in a book review, and except as permitted by U.S. copyright law.

For permissions contact:

crjaneauthor@gmail.com

milayoungarc@gmail.com

This book is a work of fiction. Names, characters, businesses, places, events, locales, and incidents are either the products of the author's imagination or used in a fictitious manner. Any resemblance to actual persons, living or dead, or actual events is purely coincidental.

Proofreading: Bookish Dream Editing

We hope you find your power, and you never let anyone take it from you.

THIEF OF HEARTS

Dark Destiny
Stolen Destiny
Broken Destiny
Sweet Destiny

BROKEN DESTINY

What happens to a siren who's come back from the dead?

I hope I get the chance to find out.
I've been betrayed, destroyed by the three men that I'd given my trust.
I'm alone again in this place… a place that's darker than hell.
And worse, something strange is happening to me.
Something that has me wondering if I can even trust myself.
There are so many secrets in these walls, and I'm now determined to find them all out.
I'm done playing nice. This siren's going to sing once again.
Nightmare Penitentiary doesn't know what's coming.
One will risk the safety of our future. One will reveal a

heartbreaking betrayal. One will bring out my own demons. And one might just be the savior I've been looking for.

Don't outstay your time at Nightmare Penitentiary. Some places you just don't survive.

CHAPTER 1

KEON

Blood.

I wanted it.

It was all I could think about.

Everything around me looked crimson through the eyes of the beast.

Somewhere in the back of my mind, I knew they were still my eyes, but when *he* took over, it literally felt like I was staring through the eyes of a stranger.

I lifted my claw up to my mouth, licking the salty blood that coated them.

Something gnawed at me. I was supposed to be paying attention to something...something other than blood.

A high-pitched whine filled my senses, like an animal was in pain.

The beast chuckled, the idea of a wounded animal had him salivating.

The scream grew louder, and I turned to see where it was coming from.

A hellhound shifter was curled up by a body, great sobs racking its body as the creature continued its mournful whine.

Intrigued, I took a step forward, shocked when the hellhound dared to jump up and growl at me, baring almost all of its razor sharp teeth.

The beast growled low in our chest as we prepared to lunge at it.

Until I saw her.

The hellhound's movement had revealed the body it had been wrapped around.

Everything came rushing at me at once. It felt like someone was taking a hammer to my skull as the last few hours burst their way through the bloody haze of the beast's mind, clearing the way for me to take my body back over.

I rushed to go to her, when the hellhound's teeth sank into my shoulder. I roared, and it took everything in me to keep the beast at bay.

"I'm not going to hurt her. Let me go!" I snarled through clenched teeth as I tried to shake him off. His teeth ripped at my sinew and muscle as I yanked at him.

I finally used my left fist to crack his skull, knocking him out and giving me blessed relief from his knife-like teeth as his jaw released my shoulder. He sank to the floor, and I shook out my arm. It hurt like a motherfucker, and I knew my whole right side wouldn't be useable for several hours as my healing powers kicked in.

The agonizing pain in my shoulder faded away as I sank by Selena's side, horror breaching every cell in my body as I realized that she wasn't just unconscious. She had no pulse.

But that fact should have been obvious to me as I'd ripped out her fucking throat. Blood seeped from the wound. Her blue tipped hair was a macabre purple and pink color, stained from all the blood she'd lost.

My whole body shook as I stared at her. Flashbacks of every time I'd touched her perfect skin, every time I'd felt her perfect lips. The way she sighed as she said my name.

This girl was my fucking everything. Her mark was on my soul, the same as my mark was on her skin.

My head sank back as I roared at the flickering lights in the ceiling above me. My mind raced as I tried to think of something that could be done. I'd do anything…give anything to save her.

Alaric. The mob asshole's face filled my mind.

He would know what to do. He had to know what to do. Everyone knew he had power that others didn't. The rumors were that he'd wanted to come to Nightmare Penitentiary, he hadn't been forced to.

I was afraid to move Selena, in case my jostling did more internal damage, but I was more afraid of leaving her here with the hellhound unconscious and who knows what lurking around the halls. The appearance of the beast had scared off all of the bystanders I could faintly recall at the start of the fight. But still...

This prison was aptly named.

And how much more damage could I do dragging her around if she was dead?

I gently picked her up with my left arm, draping her legs over my right arm, even though it was still in bad shape. I raced through the hallways, the familiar paths seeming like labyrinths in my panicked state.

"Hold on, sweetheart," I whispered into her hair, the tang of blood hiding her usual smell. When I was a child, my grandmother had talked about a waiting place that immortals went to after they died, a place where they were judged before being sent to Heaven or Hell.

I didn't know if I believed in Heaven. And I was pretty sure that Nightmare Penitentiary was at least a part of Hell. But I was desperate to believe there was a waiting place. Because maybe if that existed, then she could come back.

Even if it didn't exist though, I'd break through the gates of Heaven to get her soul back to Earth.

The beast inside of me snarled at the thought.

After what felt like hours, but must have been minutes, I made it to Alaric's hell.

He was pacing, anxiety engrained into his features.

"Selena," he cried out as he ran towards the bars and shook them like he had the power to rip them apart.

The warden had made sure he didn't.

"What the fuck did you do to her, you fucking

bastard?" Alaric seethed, the whites of his eyes disappearing as he began to lose control.

"She's dead," I said flatly, even though the words threatened to shred the very inside of my soul as I uttered them.

"What?" Alaric's voice came out choked as he tried to comprehend what I'd just said. Even now, Selena's blood was dripping to the floor beneath her, the wound too ragged and large to be stopped.

"I…I ripped her throat out when I transformed."

I knew that Alaric knew what I was talking about. Part of his power was to know everyone's secrets. So I had no doubt that he knew mine.

"I need you to fix her. Bring her back. Now!" I ordered, shaking Selena a bit in my arms as I struggled for control.

Setting her down as gently as I could, I pulled out the key, unlocked the door, and threw open the cell.

Alaric just stared at Selena as if he was in a daze.

I pushed him back onto the cell bars, and his head snapped back against the metal, sending a loud clang echoing through the hallways.

"Help her," I roared.

He tore his eyes away from Selena and stared at me, his gaze crazy and desperate.

"I can't bring her back from the dead," he whispered to me.

Now it was my turn to stare at him blankly. I didn't understand what he was saying. Of course he could bring her back. There was no other option. There wasn't another creature more powerful in these walls besides the warden himself. There was no one else I could turn to.

I released Alaric and shakily stepped away. Alaric sank to the ground and gathered Selena's body in his arms, his entire body trembling as he murmured words to her I was too messed up to hear.

My claws extended, digging into my face as I roared. I could just let go, there wasn't a reason to hold on anymore. This was all my fault.

"The fae," Alaric suddenly cried, springing to his feet with Selena still in his arms. He took off down the hallway before I could fully comprehend what he'd just said.

The haze that was threatening to take completely over rapidly dissipated once again, and I took off after him, our thunderous footsteps filling the hallway.

I felt the gaze of prisoners as they warily watched us fly by. Alaric was going so fast that it was hard for even me to catch up to him.

My thoughts raced as we ran towards where they were keeping the fallen fae prince.

The fae were powerful, that couldn't be denied. And their power was ancient, so ancient that nothing was really known about what they could do.

But as I'd said before, if someone was going to know about another supernatural's secrets, it would be Alaric.

A small tendril of hope began to swirl inside of me, despite how hard I was trying to tamp it down.

How long had she been dead now? Thirty minutes? An hour? I couldn't be sure how much time passed when the beast had taken over. I strained my brain, trying to think about if supernaturals suffered from brain damage like humans or if Selena's healing powers would make that a non-issue.

And now my thoughts were just going down a rabbit hole, because I couldn't think about the actual reality in front of me—that every second that passed was a second closer to her never opening her eyes again.

Alaric bypassed where the guards would usually turn to get towards the fae's cell and instead ran down one more corridor before stopping abruptly. He muttered to himself as he held Selena with one arm and pressed on a few of the rocks in the wall. I wasn't surprised when an opening silently appeared in front of us, even though this route wasn't familiar to me.

This fucking place seemed to grow secret passageways overnight. The warden had said as much during guard orientation. He'd said that Nightmare Penitentiary was a living creature, and I hadn't ever seen anything to the contrary.

Alaric headed into the black void of the tunnel, and I followed him without hesitation. I pulled out the flashlight in my pocket and turned it on, almost dropping it when Alaric hissed at me. "Turn that fucking thing off, do you want to wake them up?"

He didn't bother telling me what he didn't want to wake up, and I didn't ask. The flashlight went back into my pocket, and I concentrated on listening to Alaric's footsteps as he ran, trying to follow him while not running into him.

Despite the fact that we were running through a tunnel basically blind, in half the time it would have taken to get to the fae's cell on the other route, Alaric stopped and fumbled with what must have been a wall in front of him.

Dim lighting appeared, and Alaric and I strode through into the decrepit hallway where the fae and the other prisoners the warden desired to torture were kept.

Before the wall could close behind me, I looked back and saw what looked like several pairs of red, glowing eyes staring out after us.

I probably wouldn't be using that tunnel as a regular passageway in the future.

"Fae," Alaric spat as we approached his cell, one of Selena's arms dangling beneath her like a limp doll.

The fae was lying on his bed per usual, beat to a bloody pulp. He rolled over with a groan, only half-heartedly sparing us a glance.

His whole body flinched when he realized that it was Selena in Alaric's arms.

I'd been jealous of Selena's feelings for the fae from the very beginning. The looks she gave him were softer, the feelings she had for him had always seemed truer than the ones she held for me. I'd even contemplated killing him a few times when I'd followed her and watched them together.

I was so glad that I held off the compulsion right now, as Seth hurriedly dragged himself off the cot and stumbled his way towards the cell doors, his gaze locked on Selena.

I unlocked the door and ripped it open. Alaric was through the cell door before Seth had taken more than a few steps. He gently laid her down on the blood and sweat-stained cot. For a moment, I was caught off guard by the tender look he was giving her.

He loved her.

It was written across his face. He didn't just love her. She was everything to him.

My inner beast roared at the thought.

Mine, mine, mine, it screamed, even though its obsession had led to her downfall.

I could have left her alone after that night in the bar, never stalked her down the hallways of the prison or watched her every night as she slept.

"What happened?" Seth choked out. There was no color in his face as he gazed down at her with dread.

"She's dead. You need to bring her back," Alaric ordered, taking over since I seemed to have lost the ability to speak. "And don't say you can't," he said, cutting off whatever Seth was about to say.

The beast growled inside of me again at the thought that Seth would refuse to help. He'd be dead if those words left his mouth.

"I'd never," Seth whispered as he gave Selena a longing look. "But I need..." His voice trailed off as he began to pat down Selena's prison jumpsuit anxiously.

"What are you doing?" Alaric snarled.

"The crystal. I can't do anything without it. I had her keep it for me since they're always searching my cell." Seth let out a sigh of relief as he pulled a crystal I vaguely remembered seeing in the warden's office out of her lower pocket.

"Can you do it? Can you bring her back?" I was finally able to spit out.

But Seth didn't answer me. He was already muttering something over Selena's body as he glided the crystal across her chest.

Alaric came to stand next to me. "What kind of power does he have that could bring someone back to life?" I asked him. There weren't a lot of fae that ever found themselves in this place. The fae ruled them-selves, so the fact that they'd sent one of their own to Nightmare Penitentiary, their crown prince, said a lot for the crime they'd thought he committed.

"It's something only fae royalty are said to be able to do. Through that crystal, they're able to connect to the afterlife, where the fae royals' ancestors suppos-edly reside. They drag the souls through the connection."

"But..." I responded, sensing that he wasn't saying something.

"But just because he gets her soul back doesn't mean that she'll live again," he said quietly. "The soul still has to choose to return back to earth."

We were both silent after that. Why would Selena choose to come back to the hell that had been her life on earth? Her last memory had been of me slicing her throat open.

There was no chance.

I had to look away from Seth and Selena. I staggered my way over to the wall and slid down it, my hands on my face. I was heartbroken, unable to breathe. My body began to shake, and I closed my eyes, desperate for the escape the beast could bring.

Suddenly, a gasped breath filled the cell, followed by the sound of coughing and an anguished cry from Alaric. I sprang to my feet and sprinted over to the bed, where Selena was staring wildly at the three of us as we all gaped down at her.

I couldn't believe what I was seeing, even though her stunning eyes filled to the brim with tears was all the proof I should have needed. My heart was beating wildly in my chest as I saw that her once ravaged neck was now perfectly smooth, like nothing had ever happened.

The fae suddenly collapsed next to us, and Alaric barely caught him in time. His breathing was out of control, but I couldn't spare him a glance.

Selena's body started to tremble. "What..." she croaked. I reached out to her and then quickly pulled away. I didn't deserve to touch her. She might not remember what happened right now, but when she did...

She'd never want anything to do with me again.

But at least she'd be alive. At least I could exist, knowing she was still in the world.

Selena began to sob and thrash wildly. I froze, not knowing what to do.

"You're back with us. Everything is going to be all right. Seth brought you back," Alaric said, trying to soothe her, but his words seemed to make her even more hysterical.

Footsteps echoed down the hallway. I had a lot of sway in this place, but I didn't have a good reason why I was in the fae's cell with two other prisoners. I didn't want the warden asking questions.

"We need to get her out of here," I whispered urgently, picking her up quickly as the footsteps drew closer. My right arm had finally healed, making the process much smoother.

It was hard to keep my arms from tightening around her in relief at the feel of her soft body against mine. She'd been so cold before as I'd carried her around the hallway, and now here she was, breathing against me, warm and alive.

Alaric strode after me as I hurriedly left the cell. He looked back at Seth, who was sitting on the ground, looking like he could faint at any minute. "I owe you," he said gruffly.

The guards were coming from the passageway I knew about, so once again, I found myself going through Alaric's pitch-black tunnel, except this time, there was a tendril of fear that spiked through my stomach. I knew the beast could kill whatever monsters were hiding in the dark, but I couldn't risk losing control again.

I just hoped that Alaric knew what he was doing.

I breathed a sigh of relief when we made it through. And I didn't bother looking back this time. I could feel those red eyes watching me the entire time we'd walked through the tunnel.

The corridor was thankfully empty, and we made it back to Selena's cell just in time for her cries to erupt into full-on shrieks.

I froze as she grew more and more hysterical. Alaric took her gently out of my arms and laid her down on the bed. Her cries lessened, but she was still trembling wildly.

I watched as he climbed into the cot with her, wrapping his arms around her body as she buried her face into his chest.

I stared at them for a long moment, abject longing filling up my soul. I stayed there watching her like I had from almost the moment I'd met her.

Except I didn't feel that I had a right to it now.

I finally dragged myself back to my room, a mixture of dread and relief churning in my gut.

She was alive. But I'd probably lost her forever.

But at least she was alive.

CHAPTER 2

SELENA

$\mathcal{I}$ inhaled sharply, bolting upright in bed, utterly lost.

Cement walls, filthy floor, and a metal barred entrance. I sat unmoving as flashes of memories came back to me, bursting across my mind.

Pop. Pop. Pop.

Prison. I tried to remember everything.

The word hovered in my mind as all the pieces slotted back into their place in my mind like a puzzle. I closed my eyes and leaned forward, waiting for a faint buzzing sound in my head to stop. What was that? I glanced around, reminded of a fly trap that constantly hummed, but couldn't see what caused the noise.

My tongue snaked out and licked my cracked lips while a deep hunger roused in me with a heavy craving for a cheeseburger. Salivating, I pushed my legs out of the bed, and my feet touched the cold floor. Typical that the one thing I craved after dying was a burger. It must be said that if the afterlife didn't have greasy burgers, well, that would suck just as much as me not remembering a single thing from the afterlife.

I'd died!

The reality crashed into me, wave after wave, and it was hard to make sense of how to deal with that.

I'd been dead, they told me, the three men who ultimately lead to my death. Three men who I had no intention of wasting another second on after everything they did to me.

I sighed and looked out through the bars of my locked door to where another inmate strolled past, minding her own business. She looked upset, probably for good reason, this whole institution had a way of draining every thread of happiness out of all of us. I grounded my teeth, hating this prison, hating Julian for putting me in here, hating every day I had to push myself out of bed in this hell.

That was when I noticed the stainless steel tray with food on the table at the end of my bed. I hurried over and brought it back on the bed with me, needing to gorge myself and forget everything.

I'd never been so hungry in my life. I scooped the mac and cheese into my mouth with the plastic spoon. The tastes exploded over my tongue like somehow my taste buds had been reawakened as well. I ate faster, unable to get enough. The chocolate pudding melted on my tongue, and I closed my eyes as the delicate taste flooded me. This had to be the most incredible thing I'd ever eaten. Had the prison gotten a new cook?

"That good is it?" a deep voice asked.

I jerked my head up to find Alaric outside my cell, one hand gripping a bar, the other deep in the pocket of his orange prison pants. His dark hair sat swept off his face, bringing out his piercing steel gray eyes. I couldn't deny everything about him called to me, especially how strong and broad he stood. He was the epitome of the ideal man no woman could deny, except I refused to give in to him and his incubus allure ever again.

Just seeing him again tightened my stomach, and the pain behind his eyes betrayed his cool demeanor.

Like everyone else in this place, he'd betrayed me. I'd heard him in the warden's office, talking about Seth's scepter. And funny how just earlier, he had asked me about the same artifact. His words spun in my mind. *If Seth says anything about the scepter, come to me before you say anything to the warden.* What game was he playing? Did he want it for himself or to present it to the warden as a favor to get something? Either way, I didn't care. He'd used me, and there was no way in hell I would tell him anything I found out.

That same heaviness twisted through me again to know I didn't mean as much to him as I had initially hoped. I hated that he made me feel this way, or that I let myself believe his intentions. Except he was there when I woke up with the other two, he'd helped me… somehow. But did that make him less guilty of using me?

I eyed him and spooned more pudding into my mouth. "What do you want?"

"I was worried about you, gorgeous." His words sounded genuine, but were they really? I wasn't sure what to believe.

I lowered my head back to my empty tray. Damn, where had all my food gone so fast?

"Can I get you more pudding?"

I met his gaze again, those stunning steel gray eyes that always make me forget myself…they were always getting me in trouble. My head wasn't feeling right, the buzzing refusing to abate, and I didn't want to deal with him. And as tempted as I was to give in, just for another few bites of sweets, I couldn't forget his betrayal.

"I just need to be alone, please."

"Did I do something wrong?" he asked, tilting his head to the side, and I could see his knuckles starting to go white from how hard he gripped the metal bar.

I frowned, my chest bubbling with words I wanted to throw at him, but my head wasn't feeling right. And I didn't want to get into an argument with me feeling this way. At the end of the day, I freaking died because I got close to dangerous men who'd hidden secrets from me, and that meant being smarter about how I dealt with them going forward.

"I want some time alone."

"I'm here for you, baby," he said.

I blinked at him, unsure how to take that. Was I just a means for him to find out information, or was the look in his eyes sincere? Part of me wanted to slow-clap him for his act, yet part of me didn't want to get into an argument and listen to more lies.

Setting the empty food tray on the floor near my bed, I got back under the covers and curled in on myself, trying to shut out the humming sound in my ears.

Part of me felt bad for pushing him away. After all, he had broken into the warden's office and retrieved Seth's crystal for me, except was that some set up too? A ploy to win me over to find out about the scepter? I didn't know, but I had to remind myself I refused to be anyone else's stepping stone anymore. Not to mention, I'd died!

Closing my eyes, I pushed everything aside, attempting to not let it faze me.

"I'll let you sleep then. I'll come see you later," he said, and his footfalls faded.

"Don't bother," I whispered back, unsure if he heard me.

I didn't know how much time had passed when someone calling my name woke me up.

"Selena," he said again, and only then did it become clear who spoke.

Keon. I froze on my bed, curled up, unsure how to respond.

He'd kept secrets from me from the beginning, secrets about him being a demon, secrets that ended up getting me killed.

"Are you awake, sweetheart?"

When I heard his voice, images of him changing as he fought the hellhound inmate, Laz, swept over my mind. One after another, they kept coming.

Cold black eyes.

Clawed hands.

Horns pushing out from his temples.

And that wasn't the part that scared me. It was the look in his eyes when he turned on me. There was no sign of Keon inside, only a starved monster who saw me as a meal. Then he attacked me...killed me.

How could I not have known about that side of him?

I curled in tighter on myself and hoped with every fiber of my body that he didn't come in. He was a guard so he had access, but I hoped he respected me enough to give me space.

"I don't know if you're awake," he began. "But I want to explain everything to you. I feel like fucking shit at how things turned out. That's not who I am." He sighed loudly, his voice gravelly and remorseful. "I'd do anything to protect you, and what I did to you is killing me."

Trembling, I lay in bed, unmoving, feeling powerless, wanting to state that obviously, he *had* killed me. I couldn't avoid him for long. Except making sense of the fear, the hurt, the anger left me numb, and I couldn't face him. Not yet. Not until I sorted myself out. Our encounters together had always been scorching hot and imprinted on my mind. It shocked me how much he affected me, not to mention, somehow, he'd marked me, leaving two stars on my ankle. Who the hell was this guy anyway? Sometimes, I wonder if it was a coincidence that I picked him out of all the guys at the bar to give my virginity to what felt like a lifetime ago.

Thinking back, I'd been too naïve, which ended up with everyone walking all over me. Including Julian and even my own mother. I had no intention of repeating my past mistakes. I'd died and came back, which meant this was my second chance, right?

"I'll let you be," Keon murmured, his voice deflated. "We'll speak later," he promised me, and I had no doubt about that, except determination curled in my chest.

I didn't hear him walking away, but I refused to look up, just in case he remained outside my cell, and instead, I welcomed sleep as it finally feathered around the edges of my sight. Falling into sleep came fast and snatched me away.

I opened my eyes to the sound metal clicking...the familiar noise of my prison cell door unlocking.

Panic wrenched through me, and I scrambled out of bed, half expecting to find Keon making his way inside. Except, he wasn't there. No one was...the doors were on an automatic sensor to open up that way every morning.

I sighed and rubbed my eyes. "How long have I been sleeping?" I mumbled to myself.

Outside in the corridor, inmates started emerging from their cells and making their way to the bathroom or mess hall, I guessed. Speaking of which, I was in major need of a wash, so not wasting another second, I grabbed clean clothes and shoes from the shelf at the back of my room. Quickly, I headed to the communal showers. I recognized many of the other prisoners, mostly females who, like me, preferred to wash before the men came in.

On fast steps, I finally arrived in the bathroom and made quick work to grab a towel and head into the cubical in the corner. Less likely of people walking past and poking their head inside.

I drew the flimsy plastic curtain shut and undressed, then I dumped the dirty clothes in a pile. I flung the towel and fresh clothes over the curtain railing. Turning around, I switched on the water. Cold water sprayed over my body, but I wasn't complaining.

While I washed in ultra-fast mode, memories hovered at the edges of my mind just before I died. Afterward, there was nothing but darkness. I searched deeper through my thoughts as though there was something I had forgotten... Something just out of reach.

Nothing.

Why couldn't I remember anything from the afterlife? I had read so many articles and seen shows about people experiencing a white light or something when they died. Disappointment slithered over me at not recalling anything.

Except, I wasn't exactly the same now, was I?

Food tasted like I was eating it for the first time. The constant humming in my ears, like the television was left on a static channel, continued. Then there was that sensation that I didn't quite fit in my skin. That was a stupid way of explaining it, but the strange sensation lingered.

A coldness sank deep into my bones at the thought that I'd come back different. I'd read *Pet Cemetery* enough times to know things went askew when death was involved. A tremble raced down my spine. Clearly, I was overthinking this and letting it get to me. What I needed were actual facts. And that meant paying the library a visit and reading up on other death-like encounters. But first, I had to check into the kitchen to see if I was on shift work. Not like I could sit around overthinking everything until it drove me crazy.

By the time I'd dried myself and gotten dressed, I started to feel some level of normalcy. I made a quick pit stop in my cell to comb my wet hair and apply deodorant and then marched into the mess hall. The whole time, I scanned the hallways for any sign of Keon, terrified he'd come out and drag me into a room to talk. But that was the last thing I desired. Throwing myself into work sounded like the perfect solution.

Inmates already strolled into the room, lining up for their breakfast. From the corner of my eye, I scanned them for any familiar faces. My heart thumped in my chest that I might see Alaric, but he wasn't there. I rushed past and headed to the door near the food station against the back wall, where I normally collected my cart for delivery. It wasn't there.

My stomach growled at the delicious aroma of toast.

The door suddenly opened, and Boris, the head chef, emerged, wearing a blue apron, his long hair drawn into a ponytail. His gaze met mine, and upon recognizing me, his eyes narrowed. He looked angry. I cringed, well aware of what was coming.

"You're late," he barked, drawing attention from several inmates nearby lining up for their meal.

"I'm sorry. I-I—"

He sneered, then a softness washed over his expression. "Heard what happened to you, so I'll overlook it this time only. Don't be late again."

I nodded. "Of course."

"Get in the kitchen and load your cart. Trevor's waiting to take you into maximum security to deliver meals. You better hurry. The inmates will be starved."

And I did just that, figuring I could sneak in something to eat from the kitchen. Though I found it interesting I was back on food delivery to the prisoners underground, instead of focusing on Seth. The warden must have given Boris new instructions. Fine by me. Down there, I just delivered food and was mainly left alone.

Half the day flew past, and it surprised me when we arrived back into the mess hall and lunch was already being prepared. I helped myself to a bowl of tomato soup with chunks of stale bread that were a poor excuse for croutons and sat at a table near the window where a sliver of light poured in from outside. The soup tasted like fresh tomatoes with a layer of basil, thick and sliding like silk on my tongue. I moaned with delight and kept eating, well aware this stuff came out of a huge metal can and had tasted like crap in the past. Still, I couldn't get enough.

A shadow fell over me. I glanced up to find some bald guy with ink up his arms and neck, standing across from me.

"Been watching you. If you keep eating your soup like you're having an orgasm, my friends and I can make it a dream come true." He winked at me and peered over his shoulder at the table with two other men.

Suddenly, I lost my appetite and got to my feet. "Get the fuck away from me."

Not waiting for a response, I marched out of there, their laughter following me out into the corridor. Assholes.

CHAPTER 3

KEON

I leaned over the railing, staring down into the main prison area, my gaze locked on Selena. I'd been watching her ever since she left her cell in the morning. Rushing about, looking over her shoulder constantly, but I wasn't a damn fool.

She was scared of me and keeping her distance. I clenched my fists, loathing how damn wrong the fight against Laz had gone. My inner demon took over, a monster I'd lived with all my life. I was born this way and spent my whole life trying to hide him from the world. His hunger was ravenous, and the only way to control him was to let him out occasionally to sate that need for bloodshed. It was one of the reasons I took this job at Nightmare Penitentiary. Who'd miss a few missing pieces of scum? The worst of the worst resided here, and some of those asshats deserved a far worse punishment than just being locked up.

But all of that meant shit and was no excuse for what I did to Selena.

Nothing I'd ever done filled me with the kind of passion she roused in me, with how she made me feel alive after years of living like an empty shell. Then I'd gone and destroyed it all.

Fuck.

Sickness churned in my gut, and I felt like I was going to throw up. Except I'd already done that earlier, and my stomach was still empty. Now I bled on the inside at the agony pulsing within me.

I growled under my breath, while fury burned through me. My sanity wore thin.

I'd killed Selena. Nothing I did would change that.

There was no other way to look at it.

I'd fucked up so severely, and I don't know how to come back from the mess.

I glanced down at her as she pushed her empty cart into the mess hall, her dark hair with blue tips draped half-way down her back. Trevor strolled behind her, his eyes on her ass. Jealousy spiked, and my first reaction had me twisting toward the stairs to make him pay, to rip his eyes out and wear them as ornaments.

"What the fuck, man?" I murmured to myself. It was me I was pissed at, and I just wanted to desperately feel something other than the shame and guilt tearing me apart.

Rage slipped down to my fingertips, the beast in me pushing for release, sensing my own anger. Shouting came from the passage to my right, where a bunch of pricks were fighting. I lifted my head and sniffed the air, picking up the scent of blood.

That was my calling, and there was no holding me back. I wanted a fight, and the universe delivered. I bolted toward the gathering crowd, my footsteps thumping the hard floor.

Muffled cries emerged.

My adrenaline soared.

I threw myself into the crowd, shoving them aside, pushing them out of my way. In the middle, two men were fighting, one straddling the other, pummeling his face. Normally, I'd sit back and let them play this out. Plus, it offered entertainment, but not today. I needed this more than them, they just didn't know it.

Lunging forward, I tackled the barrel of a man on top, taking him down, my fist colliding with his head before he even hit the ground.

Darkness moved through me, my beast feeding off my raging adrenaline, pushing me to spill more blood. I wanted to listen to him, to sink deep into his energy and let him take charge. To shake that ache deep inside me, the regret chewing me alive.

But what then?

No, that was a dangerous route to fall into, so instead, I'd charge my inner assault with fists and aggression. This emotion I could cope with. Anything else was a noose around my neck.

Seth

THE WALLS of my prison seemed to close in around me, suffocating me. Each breath was a struggle. Up on my feet, I paced to the shut door and back to my bed, the quiet giving way to thoughts slowly chipping away at me.

Each time I closed my eyes, all I saw were images of Selena lying on the bed, dead. A soft light had spilled on her face, breaking the darkness consuming her. I shattered into a thousand pieces to see her gone. So I did the only thing possible to bring her back.

But even after that, she'd made her decision to pull away from me. Of course she would. I'd caught her spying on me kissing Alania. I ground my back molars, digging my nails into my palms until they broke skin. Maybe all the torture I'd received had changed me. Now I longed to feel anything but the agony of her catching me.

I huffed loudly and punched a wall, my knuckles scraping the hard surface, tearing skin. She wasn't meant to see me. Alania meant nothing to me. She was a means to an end, a role I had to play to protect my family lineage. She was all I had left from home, and I couldn't risk lacerating that connection.

My world darkened without Selena's presence, with her pulling away from me, but I couldn't risk what was best for my kingdom. For the safety of so many innocents.

It didn't change the cold hard fact that she would no

longer want me. It destroyed me to know I hurt her and that she may never forgive me. But I'd ended up in this shithole because I'd been set up, and so much depended on my survival. That was my goal, not falling for a siren.

Seething, I returned to my pacing, unsure of my next steps with Selena, unsure how long I could torture myself this way. Did I tell her the truth, risking the news reaching the warden?

Muffled voices echoed outside my prison, and I jerked my head up to the door. A couple of men walked past, deep in heavy whispers. It wasn't Selena. Of course it wouldn't be.

I moved away from the door and to my bed, where I flopped down. Selena's voice filled my head, and for a moment, she was standing in front of me, delivering the crystal she'd claimed back from the warden.

I'm sorry that you were ever parted with it to begin with, she had said.

She'd risked so much to get the crystal back for me. And the way she had looked at me with those beautiful blue eyes reminded me of the sky back home. Unblemished and bewitching. I'd tried so hard to push her away from me, so when had she crawled into my heart?

I fisted my hands, hating that I cared about her pulling away from me.

The metal click of my door unlocking echoed through the silence.

They were coming for me. My torturers.

I stiffened, my heart pounding loudly like it was trying to escape.

Two guards marched inside, wearing grins like they always did when they came to take me to get whipped. I tried to swallow, but I pushed up to my feet, ready to drown in excruciating pain to forget everything else.

Whatever Selena and I had was over. I had to accept that, even as the heaviness of that loss filled me with dark thoughts.

"It's time," the man with a hooked nose declared, lifting his hand with the shackles.

I didn't fight them but raised my arms, offering them my wrists. I'd learned long ago that no matter what I did, the torture still continued. I stepped forward, and they snapped the black cuffs on, then wrenched me outside the prison cell.

I had to focus on my task, and distractions like Selena would only get me killed. It was horrific to learn Keon killed her accidently. Idiotic fool. Except, that shouldn't be my concern now that she was alive. I did what I could for her, gave her more than I should have any human.

What mattered was my kingdom.

My family.

My realm.

And that meant sacrificing myself and everything that was dear to me, including Selena.

Alaric

I DELIVERED one punch after another to his gut, sending him sprawling to the ground. "Do you yield?" I bellowed, my whole body shuddering with range as I bounced on my toes.

Liam stared up at me, one eye bloody, his lip busted, and he grimaced when he tried to move his arm. I was sure I'd dislocated his shoulder. "Yes, fuck, man! I yield, psychopath."

I let his comment pass as two of his cronies rushed onto the court and dragged him away.

"Who's next?" I called out, pivoting on the spot to scan the outdoor yard encased by a metal fence on three fronts and the entrance back inside the penitentiary dead ahead. Most of the spectators sat on the stairs, filling their miserable sad days with betting on these fights.

We'd often held fights outside to solve problems or other times for entertainment. Right now, I needed to blow off steam before I combusted.

"No one is taking up the challenge? I'm offering you the chance to try to beat the shit out of me."

The dozen inmates sitting around watching didn't say a word. Fucking chicken shits, the lot of them.

I tensed, my jawline clenching, needing to fight, to take out my aggression. Anything to get my mind off Selena.

That asshole, Keon, had killed her. Goddamn demon. It was him I wanted to face out here and destroy. What burned me further was knowing how much he cared for Selena. I'd seen it on his face when he brought her to me—the panic, the dread of losing something so precious, he wasn't sure he could go on.

Fire swallowed me that she meant so much to him, and same with that fucking fae. She was mine, and I wanted to rip them apart for touching her.

Except, that wasn't an option, especially after my visit to her yesterday, when she'd pushed me away. What the fuck was that about?

I'd tried to save her.

I wrenched from the memory and turned to a mountain of a man strolling toward me. Trunks for arms, head shaved bald, and by the wings inked on the side of his neck, I could tell he was part of the eagle shifter gang. You'd be surprised how corrupt these feathery pricks were, and it explained why there were at least twenty of them in the penitentiary.

I smirked and cracked my neck. "About fucking time." A challenge to throw myself into.

"Heard you've got a death-wish over losing out on pussy," he growled.

I lifted my gaze to his ugly mug. Large jaw, pointy nose, and beady eyes. I was going to rearrange his face for spewing such bullshit in front of me.

"Be careful what rumors you spread. I don't take well to bullshit. Get your fucking facts right." What pissed me off worse was that the shit that just fell from his mouth would be on everyone's lips. The rumor mill would be on fire in the penitentiary, and well, I had every intention of correcting that error.

Starting with this creep.

"You know what they say," he droned on. "Where there's smoke, there's fire. Maybe instead of throwing punches, go work out your shit with the girl."

What the fuck? "Stop talking, you snot-sucking bastard. You going to whine like a goddamn shrink or fucking fight?"

I swear these bird shifters loved nothing more than listening to their own voices.

He pushed the sleeves of his orange jumpsuit up to his elbows. "Fine, you pissy scum sack. You want insults and a fight to deal with your emotions, let's do this."

I rolled my eyes. "Seriously. Even when you try to insult me, you sound like a cunt. You're ruining this for me."

He laughed, chortling like a hyena. And that was the limit of my patience. The sound was like razor blades down my back.

Anger lashed over me, and my growl deepened, turning feral.

As he kept mocking me, I curled my hands into fists and threw myself at him. He anticipated my move, and in a flash, his wings ripped out from the back of his shirt, large feathery gray things. He pivoted on the spot, a wing whacking into me with such force, it threw me off my course and I stumbled sideways.

I heaved each breath and jerked my head to the bird

brain. His dark eyes glinted in the daylight, and he looked up for a split second as a wild falcon flew past. Yeah, he'd love nothing more than to fly up and join him, if it weren't for the invisible currents way overhead. They'd zap him to death the moment he touched them. That would be a sight to behold.

Grinning, I straightened myself, seeing the ass was going to play dirty. Perfect. That was exactly how I preferred my battles. We circled each other, while the crowd cheered. What pissed me off about him more than anything was that he touched on a soft spot that rang too close to home. And it was shit enough, I didn't need someone else poking holes in my misery.

I'd get Selena back, I was under no misconception there, but how long it would take was another story.

First, get rid of my rage and teach this bastard a lesson. My demonic side teetered just below the surface, and the first wisps of smoke curled out from the corners of my mouth. Two could play at this game.

He unleashed a bird-like shriek.

"That's right, you'll be screaming for pity soon enough," I said, tossing the words at him.

Then we lunged for each other and collided in a massive clash. Only darkness consumed me, and this was exactly what I'd been seeking—a battle to lose myself in.

CHAPTER 4

SELENA

*L*istless.

That's how I felt.

I should have been rejoicing for every day that I was alive.

I was a stranger in my skin since I'd woken up, and every day, it seemed to get worse.

I hated them. I loved them.

I never wanted to see them again.

Or at least that's what I told myself.

But they were everywhere. I could feel their presence.

They'd all become my stalkers. For days, I'd kept my distance, but I always felt their eyes on me.

Well, at least Alaric and Keon had. Seth was trapped in his cell, but I had no doubt he would join the others if he could. Every time I passed food to his section of the prison, he stared at me. He'd occasionally pepper me with questions, but for the most part, he just stared as if he were trying to see all the way into my soul.

And maybe he could. He could bring people back from the dead, after all.

I hadn't said thank you to him. Right now, I honestly wasn't sure if I was thankful.

Everything was a blur from when I'd died, but somewhere in the back of my mind, I knew that I'd chosen to come back to this life.

I just didn't know why.

I picked at my food in the cafeteria, aware of the eyes that were watching me.

A prison was worse than a pack of teenage girls when it came to rumors. Word had quickly gotten out that Keon had killed me, and yet somehow, here I was. No one seemed to have heard about Seth's role in all of it.

Which was a good thing for him. I didn't think the fae would appreciate it if it became common knowledge that their royals could bring people back from the dead. Supernaturals would be doing whatever they could to break down the gates into Faerie and raise their loved ones.

I took a bite of mashed potatoes, wincing at their watery taste, my tastebuds not what they were earlier. With the way I was feeling though, I doubt a steak from a five-star restaurant on the outside would taste any different.

Alaric stalked into the cafeteria. The entire atmosphere of the room changed as everyone looked his way. A gaggle of female prisoners tittered nervously as he passed by their table, I'm sure all of them hoped they would get a chance in his bed today.

But he didn't pay them any attention. His gaze was locked on me.

Goodie.

"What do you want, Alaric?" I asked wearily as he sat down in the seat in front of me.

I was really going to need to start taking my meals in my cell. I was less likely to run into one of them there.

It was a weird thing to both crave and detest being by myself.

"You're done ignoring me," he told me bluntly, staring at me intensely.

I raised an eyebrow. "Really? I didn't know that was your decision to make."

He sighed as if I was a petulant child that he needed to lecture.

"I don't know why you're acting like this. I helped *save* your life. You're treating me the same as that guard of yours, and it makes no fucking sense."

The phrase "guard of yours" made me cringe.

I was trying not to think about the fact that Keon had ever possibly been mine. Because if I thought about that, and the ways that Alaric and Seth had both betrayed me as well, then I would have to admit that I had the worst taste in men possible.

And I really didn't want to admit that right now.

"See! You can't even think about him. I can understand that reaction, but I'm done with you putting distance between us. I've let you have your time to sulk. This is done." His eyes darkened menacingly as he stared at me, as if he could will his way into changing my mind. His eyes were more like flint than their usual glittering silver, and I forced myself not to shiver under his gaze.

He gave a low, short, frustrated growl when my face remained impassive despite his little speech.

I may have looked calm on the outside, but inside, I was fuming.

He didn't know why I was ignoring him...

That was hilarious. It made me feel a bit powerful in the moment to know that I had one on this powerful incubus, who usually knew everything that went on in the prison. I had one on all of them when I thought about it like that.

"Alaric, I have nothing to say to you right now. And you can tell the rest of the guys that applies to them as well. *If*—and when I say 'if,' that's a really big if—I choose to talk to any of you again, it will be on my terms. You can leave now."

Alaric stared at me, his mouth hanging open like I'd shocked him beyond measure. And maybe I had. I doubted that very many people ever had the nerve to stand up to him.

I wouldn't have the nerve usually, but I guess dying kind of had the effect of making you not give a fuck.

"Selena," he whispered in a voice that almost

sounded distraught. It was all I could do to keep my face impassive.

He stood up abruptly, his chair crashing to the ground behind him, garnering even more stares. "I'll give you more time, but I'm warning you, I don't have much patience left. You're mine, and there's nothing that anyone can do about that, including you."

He stalked off, rage emanating off of him, making everyone he passed shrivel in fear. There was a burnt smell in the air, like his usually delicious sex smell had been scorched by his rage.

The smell in the air could have been from my fury as well. The doors of the cafeteria slamming behind him did nothing to calm me down.

How dare he? How dare all of them!

So many stares finally became suffocating, and now it was my turn to burst out of my seat and practically sprint out of the room.

I'd made it halfway down the hall when I heard my name called.

"Selena!"

It was Laz.

I sighed and slowed down as I heard his footsteps in the hallway behind me get closer.

I felt his soft touch on my shoulder. It was a little amazing to me that a creature that held so much power could somehow be so gentle with me.

I turned to look at him, studying his gorgeous, concerned face.

I didn't want gentle right now.

What I wanted was a distraction.

And I'd bet that Laz was just the distraction I needed.

"Sel—" he began. But I was done talking.

I grabbed his face and then smashed my lips against his, briefly noting the look of shock and then lust on his face right before our lips touched.

It took a second for him to return my kiss. He made a slight groaning sound, and then he deepened the kiss. I used my tongue to trace his lips before wrapping my arms around his neck. Laz's tongue moved against mine, teasing but persistent. I opened wider for him, tasting chocolate and caramel…and something else. Something rich and masculine. Something all Lazarus.

He groaned again, his hands moving behind my head and up into my hair. He fisted it, gently tugging my head back and kissing me harder. He took control of the kiss then…and me, using his hands in my hair to move me where he wanted. Laz dropped one hand down to cup my ass before easily lifting me. I instinctively wrapped my legs around his waist, feeling him hard against me.

He carried me down the hallway without stopping.

Laz opened a door and strode into what looked like one of the shower rooms and set me down just inside the door. He pushed me up against it. I looked up into his face and felt something flicker in my chest, forgetting for a second this was just a release. There weren't any emotions involved.

No one would hear us in the tiled room. Shower

schedules were strictly adhered to here. I didn't even know how we'd managed to get in here. Apparently, Laz had the same ability as the others to work around the rules of the prison.

Ugh. The others. I wouldn't think about them. I wouldn't.

Laz was too busy undressing to notice my distraction. As he untucked the navy prison top from his pants, I caught a glimpse of his muscular abdomen before he let it drop. My breathing roughened when he removed his shirt, exposing his stomach, arms, and chest. Laz had the kind of body that looked capable of inflicting pain and pleasure equally. His scattered tattoos made him look like a cage fighter who could demolish half the men in the room but still has enough stamina afterward to satisfy a woman in bed better than they'd ever had it. His muscles shifted with every breath, like they could break free of his skin at any moment. He intimidated and aroused me all at once.

For a moment, my thoughts flicked to what it would look like for Alaric and Lazarus to go at it in the cage.

Stop it, I reminded myself.

"Strip," he said. His tone warned me not to protest, and I didn't want to. Before I could think any more, I slipped off my shirt and pulled on the drawstring of my pants, letting them slide down over my hips to pool at my feet, completely exposing my body to him. I pressed my palms against the door behind me so I wouldn't be tempted to cover myself.

Laz paused in the act of pulling off his pants, his black eyes seeming to darken even more. I found myself entranced as I stared at them. His gaze traveled down my body, and every inch of my skin heated, as if it were his hand caressing me and not just his eyes.

"Baby, I wish I had enough self-control to taste every inch of you." He pushed his pants and boxer briefs down his legs, stepped out of them, and moved toward me so fast, I gasped. Back pressed against the door, I let my gaze drop to the hand gripping his heavy erection, stroking it from root to head.

"Are you wet enough for me, Selena?"

Before I could answer, he guided his cock between my slightly parted thighs and through my cleft, dragging the head achingly slow through my wetness. He growled near the top of my head, circling my clit until I felt like I was going to scream. But he pulled himself away just as quickly, making me whimper in protest.

Then he dropped his hands to my ass and lifted me against him, lodging me between his body and the door.

"Wrap your legs around my waist." He groaned when I did as he commanded, cradling his erection against me. "I can't do anything but hard and fast. Do you understand? I want you too much."

"Yes," I whimpered. "Please."

He pushed inside me then with such force, the door behind me shook on its hinges. Tears sprang to my eyes, and I cried out, the sound mingling with his strangled groan. Pain sliced through me, sharp and quick. He was big, bigger than the others. I hadn't thought that was possible.

Clinging to his shoulders, I squeezed my eyes shut, waiting for the discomfort to subside as our harsh breathing echoed through the still room. Laz froze against me, chest heaving, and my eyes opened to meet his.

His gaze held an unspoken question.

"Please," I gasped. "I don't want you to stop."

His voice sounded strangled. "I don't think I could."

His already-stiff muscles bunched under my fingers as I stroked his neck and shoulders. Having Lazarus stop now would drive me off the deep end.

I laid kisses along his collarbone and his neck, entreating him to continue. Despite the sting I'd experienced when he first thrust into me, the way his erection filled me felt perfect now.

Pain always brought the most perfect pleasure.

Impaled by his hips against the hard surface of the door, I shifted slightly in an effort to assuage the building ache.

"Hold still." Punctuating his order, Laz's hips drove me into the door once more with a powerful thrust. "Fuck. Fuck. Just give me a fucking minute."

"No. I can't. Lazarus…please."

My thoughts had scattered with the movement of him inside me, and disjointed words began to fall from my lips.

The pain remained, but I could manage it since it was paired with the promise of something I knew would be pleasurable. I was already sensitive down there, and I knew that if I could just move a certain way against him, I could use his body to find the release I was desperate for.

Ignoring his request to remain still, I circled my hips over Laz's, moaning without restraint when that needy part of me slid against the smooth base of his erection buried deep inside me. I tightened my thighs around him and worked my lower body into a rhythm, concentrating on finding my pleasure as fast as possible.

I felt wild. Desperate. Needy. For him. For this.

I wanted to slow down and savor the moment, but my body wouldn't allow it. Only a few more grinds of my hips... My head fell back on my shoulders, anticipating my climax. Laz's hands gripped my bottom, his fingers digging in painfully. The friction I craved disappeared, and I moaned in protest, pulling on his hair in frustration.

"No, no, my little siren. That's not how this is going to go. We've barely gotten started."

Holding my body still against him, Lazarus dipped his head and took one of my nipples in his mouth and drew on it greedily. Hot pleasure shot through me, spreading through my belly and lower. I needed to move. I had to. But he wouldn't allow it.

After licking and sucking my nipple to a peak, he moved to my other breast and gave it the same torturous yet reverent treatment. I moved restlessly against the hard surface of the door, needing him to stop. Needing him to never stop. Lazarus raised his head, his heated eyes landing on my lips and staying there, pupils dilating. His breathing escalated with each passing second.

"Give me your mouth. I want your mouth." I pressed my forehead against his, suddenly feeling uneasy about kissing him any more. Isn't that what Julia Roberts said in *Pretty Woman*, that you shouldn't kiss anyone because it was too intimate?

Before I could think any harder on it, his lips fell on mine with a growl, biting, soothing, and licking. Our tongues met and tangled furiously. He forced my mouth open over and over again, demanding to be let inside. Head slanting right, then left, I let the kiss consume me, never once thinking to come up for air. As he dominated my mouth, any lingering pain disappeared, replaced with single-minded need. He felt hot and thick inside me, and my body relaxed to accommodate his size.

At some point during the kiss, Laz braced one arm against the door, wrapped the other around my waist, and mercifully, finally began moving me up and down his rigid length, slowly torturing my slick, sensitive flesh. The pace grew faster and more determined, until I was practically bouncing up and down on him.

Laz's mouth never left mine, absorbing my cries with his tongue and lips. Without warning, the pressure building inside me burst, and an immense wave of pleasure washed over me. I broke the kiss and screamed, dimly aware that Lazarus was watching me come apart in his arms as I rode out my orgasm with the use of his still-thrusting body.

When I'd finished, Lazarus buried his face in my neck with a groan. "Fuck, I'm ruined. You've ruined me, baby."

With one final thrust of his hips, he found his release. He tried to muffle his shouts against my damp skin, but they couldn't be contained, and I was too slack with pleasure to do anything but listen to the expletives he chanted against my ear.

When we finally got our breathing under control, he shifted my body around so that he could loop his arms under my knees. He gathered me against his chest, carried me towards the sinks, and then sat me down on the counter.

Please, let them just have been cleaned.

Body limp, I watched as he grabbed a towel and dampened it before he kneeled in front of me and pressed the warm cloth between my legs. I watched through half-closed eyes as he ran the cloth along my inner thighs and back up. When he'd finished his task, he tossed the cloth in one of the hampers that lined the walls and then began trailing kisses down my stomach.

My eyes flew open as the intense sensations I'd just experienced rushed back to the surface. "You know this means nothing, right?" I moaned as his warm breath drifted over me.

"Whatever you say, baby. Just let me kiss you better." Then he quickly and powerfully licked me to a second orgasm. And this time, he didn't bother to muffle my scream.

* * *

AWKWARDNESS SET in the second the euphoria from my third orgasm started to fade. The man was a god with his tongue, but his gaze, as he helped me get dressed, was too intimate. The way he softly put my hair behind my ear and then allowed his hand to linger on my cheek.

How good it felt to have him touch me like that…

No, no, no. That was not what this was.

I quickly yanked my pants back up and stepped away from him.

"Thanks for the fuck," I told him coarsely, ignoring the way his eyes shimmered in displeasure at my words.

"No problem," he said casually. I didn't miss the heat in his gaze as I shimmied my top on. Hellhounds were evidently very expressive.

"So, what was that?" he finally asked after we'd both finished dressing.

"I just needed to blow off some steam," I told him, only lying a little bit.

"Right," he said again, his body getting stiff, his voice laced with annoyance.

"I've got to go, dinner duty," I lied as I practically sprinted away.

I shook my head, trying to clear it of whatever spell that orgasm he'd just given me was.

That had to be the reason for this weird feeling in my chest.

His orgasm had done something to me.

It felt like his gaze was on me the entire way back to my cell.

And I didn't feel any better than I had before.

If anything, I felt worse.

As I lay on my cot, a burning sensation started up around my ankle. The same sensation I'd felt before.

Just like everything else about tonight, I ignored it. And what it possibly meant.

I had a feeling it wasn't going anywhere.

CHAPTER 5

SELENA

"Get up," a voice barked at me, waking me up from a night of terrible sleep.

I blearily opened my eyes to the sight of a guard leering at me from the other side of the bars.

"You've been summoned by the warden," he told me, and any residual tiredness I was feeling flew away. It had been a while since the warden had called for me, and it was never a good thing when he wanted me.

The guard wasn't as much of an asshole as some of the others around here, and he turned his back while I slipped into my uniform. He didn't say anything as he frog marched me down the hall. We were there far faster than I would have preferred. He walked off with a muttered, "Good luck," and then it was just me standing in the entryway of the warden's office, dread curling in my gut.

"Are you going to stand there all day?" the warden

growled. I took a deep breath and stepped into his office.

The warden was sitting in his desk chair, sipping a steaming red liquid from a glass cup. He didn't bother looking at me as I hesitantly walked towards the office. His focus was on the wall in front of him.

He wasn't in a good mood, that much was obvious. My nerves spiked even more.

"Well, sit down," he said exasperatedly, gesturing to the chair in front of him like I should have read his mind. I slid into the chair, sitting on the very end of it, like somehow, I'd be able to make a quick escape if things went south.

The warden finally flashed his gaze at me. "Today's your lucky day, siren. I'm going to give you your power back."

My mouth dropped open.

"Well, just for a week." He pursed his lips. "And that's always subject to change."

"I don't understand," I whispered, my heart hammering a thousand beats a minute as I leaned towards him.

"I need a favor. And you'll need your power for it. I see this as a win-win situation."

My mouth opened and then closed. I didn't see anything that was in the winning column for me. Just a taste of having my power back might be enough to finally make me crack. It had finally begun to fade, that memory of what those few hours had been like before Julian took it all.

I had no desire to be reminded of it again and start the whole process over again. A week might do me in.

"I apologize if I made it seem like you had a choice in this." He smiled and then took a long sip of his still steaming drink. "Your master will be here in five minutes. After I give you your power back, you're going to get to spend some quality time with him. I don't care how you do it, but you will convince him to give me the *rw nw prt m hrw*," he told me, his voice growing angrier.

I searched my memory, trying to remember why whatever strange name he'd just said sounded so familiar.

"*The Book of the Dead?*" I asked slowly, remembering such a book in Julian's vault.

"Very good," he said appraisingly, his gaze dancing over me. He gestured to the shelves around the room, all of them holding artifacts that were the stuff of legends. "You might have noticed I'm a bit of a collector. Julian promised me the book in exchange for some information from one of the shifter prisoners that his clan frequently quarrels with. While I fulfilled my end of the bargain, your illustrious master did not."

My spine hackled as again, he used the word "master." I wanted to scream that he'd never been my master, but I managed to keep my mouth closed.

The warden smirked like he knew exactly what I was thinking and relished my anger. Bastard.

He pulled out a pocket watch and glanced at it. "We'd better get going," he remarked before setting his drink down and striding towards the shelf where the glowing orb that held my power was kept.

The temperature in the room seemed to skyrocket as he picked it up casually before walking back towards me.

I couldn't breathe as I stared at it longingly. A part of me lay in there, and without it, I would never feel whole again.

"Go ahead, Selena. Reach out and touch it. Call it to you," he murmured, excitement gleaming in his eyes.

I dragged my gaze away from it to stare at the warden suspiciously. "This isn't some kind of joke?" I asked.

"Would I do that to you?" he answered, pretending to sound hurt.

That just pissed me off so I reached out and grabbed the orb.

Liquid lightning shot through my veins. My skin buzzed with energy as glowing light was sucked into my skin. How had I been living without this? It was like I'd been walking around half-dead ever since it was taken, and I just hadn't realized it before now. I felt… invigorated. Like I could do anything.

"Your power suits you." The warden's voice was like a dash of cold water. It sliced through my euphoria, and I was forced to come back to reality. I'd forgotten for a moment where I was.

Before I got a chance to say anything, a knock sounded on the door.

"Ah, that would be the guard telling us that our friend is here."

My power lashed out, striking at him like a whip. The warden held up a hand, and a sizzling power filled the room.

"Now, now. Let's be a good little siren," he said, as if I'd thrown confetti at him instead of trying to attack him.

A shiver crept down my spine, and my power slithered unhappily inside of me. I'd always known the warden was powerful, but the way he'd just handled that…

That was terrifying.

The warden turned his back on me, a classic power move signaling that I was no threat to him. "Come in," he called out, and a nervous-looking guard peeked his head in the room.

"Your guest is here," the man said.

"Take Selena to him. Our guest will be overjoyed at the chance for a reunion."

My whole body stiffened, and for a moment, I imagined what it would be like to launch a full-on attack, sending everything I could at the warden, at the guard, at everyone in this hellhole.

"Selena," the warden said, warning laced through his voice. I thought of how easily he'd deflected my attack, and my shoulders sunk.

"Let's go," I told the guard in a defeated voice.

The warden's cold laugh followed us all the way down the hallway.

* * *

JULIAN WAS JUST as I remembered him—silver blond hair, eyes so dark they might as well have been black, perfect skin that practically shined. The fact that a monster could be so beautiful… Somehow though, his beauty wasn't as striking as it used to be. Not after Keon, Alaric, Seth…and Laz.

His eyes widened when I walked through the door. They grew hungry as his gaze flickered over my body. I wondered what I looked like to him. Before this place, my mother had me on a very strict skin and hair regimen. My food was carefully measured, every calorie counted to make sure that I had the perfect appearance. The best I could do here was to wash my face morning and night, and makeup was nowhere to be found. My calories were probably all right, just because the slop they served here wasn't palatable most of the time and I could stomach only enough to survive.

Julian's expression didn't show any disgust, so I guessed my appearance hadn't changed that drastically. Or maybe it was my power hiding all the flaws I must have now.

The men didn't seem to have a problem, a voice in my head reminded me.

Julian's gaze grew desperate, like I was water he'd seen in the distance in the middle of the desert. "Selena," he whispered, his smooth voice coming out choked.

"Julian," I said coldly, before remembering that I was supposed to be getting something from him.

"I've missed you," he told me in a rare moment of weakness that I'd never seen from him before. I could see the self-loathing on his face the second the words came out of his mouth. Julian had always prided himself on his self-control. My mother had mentioned he'd been cracking lately…attacks on the other sirens.

"You look well," I told him evenly.

He just continued to stare at me unnervingly. I could see the hint of his fangs peeking out from his lips, meaning he was experiencing a strong emotion, or he was aroused.

It was all I could do to keep the repulsion from my face.

"Are you ready to come home? I must say, I'm impressed that you've lasted this long."

It was a strange thing. When I'd first gotten here, I'd been desperate to leave. But now there was no other choice for me but to leave on my own terms. I couldn't exchange one prison for another. And that's all Julian would ever offer me—a prison.

"I've been fine, living my best life and all of that," I told him breezily, my thoughts darting to my recent death and all the other shit I'd been through since I'd come here.

"The warden must be slacking off. I'll have to have a word with him," Julian spat, my attitude enraging him.

It hit me then how much I'd changed since I'd arrived. I wasn't the desperate, fearful girl who shrank back at the sight of her shadow. Standing in front of Julian, I no longer felt the terror that I'd once choked on every time I was in his presence.

When had that happened?

Maybe it was the fact that I'd slept with a serial killer.

I smiled at my internal monologue, only annoying Julian more.

"Care to share with the room?" he snarled.

My smile dropped.

"Did you need something from me if you aren't here to beg for my forgiveness?"

"The warden thought we might want to catch up," I told him.

Understanding flashed on his face. "He thinks you can convince me to give him the book."

I shrugged, wondering how he wasn't seeing my power. My reason for being here should have been obvious from the second I stepped in the room. Why else would my power be back?

My puzzlement over this development was pushed away when Julian started laughing. His rich, malignant laughter filled the room. Julian must be considered a special visitor, since we were all alone in the room.

My power bubbled up to the surface as his laughter continued to ring through the room. I was sure most would find his laughter attractive, after all, everything about the vampire was designed to entice...to seduce.

But to me, it might as well be nails on a chalkboard, and my power agreed.

"The warden should know by now that I can't be

swayed by pussy, even if it's the prettiest pussy I've ever seen," Julian said once his laughter had calmed down.

Disgust churned harder in my gut.

"Why did you renege on your deal?" I commented, thinking that it was a strange thing for him to have done. Julian wasn't stupid. One way that he'd become so strong was because of his ability to make alliances that benefited him. This move was out of character for him. "Isn't it in your best interest for you to have a good relationship with him?"

"I don't need anyone. And the warden should have realized that."

"Hmm," I said in a noncommittal tone, wondering if the rumors about him changing had been understated.

There was a tense silence as Julian continued to stare at me as if he was going to lunge at me and gobble me up at any second. I sneaked a look to the side, making sure there were still guards nearby just in case he did.

"How is everyone back home?" I asked, trying to distract him from whatever he was thinking.

It was his turn to hum in a noncommittal tone, and the move filled me with unease.

"Do you think about me when you're alone in your cell? Do you find yourself touching yourself as you imagine what I could do to you?"

I gaped at him, amazed at how he could be so off in the night, how he could know me so little.

"Every time I come, it's thinking of you," he said in a gravelly, thick voice laden with lust. I watched, incredulous, as his left hand drifted towards the new tent in his pants, like he wanted to rub one out right in front of me.

I'd had enough. Julian was a sicko creep and would always be a sicko creep. I didn't want to play any more games. This little task the warden had given me needed to be done, and then I never wanted to see this asshole again.

I'd seen a siren use her powers before, and although I'd only gotten a taste before, there was no time like the present to try out my powers of persuasion.

"Julian," I whispered, and the voice that came out of me was not my own. It was interlaced with a vibrant energy. It was seductive, beckoning. And then my voice cracked, and the power retracted back into me with a snap that had me stumbling back a step.

Julian shook his head and frowned. But he still didn't seem to be aware of my power. Had the warden done something to hide it?

Squaring my shoulders, I tried again. His name came out smoother this time, but just like the time before, it cracked and the spell, or whatever it was that my power did, broke.

I tried a few more times, trying to focus my energy, my calm.

And finally, Julian's name left my mouth, and this time, my voice didn't crack, not even a bit.

As soon as the word left my mouth, I knew that this vampire, even with thousands of years under his belt, wouldn't stand a chance.

"You want to fulfill your deal with the warden. It's imperative that you keep a good relationship with him. You will give him the book."

A siren had once visited from a different clan. The vampires in that clan weren't as hard on their sirens, so this one was actually quite old. She'd visited with a few of us, asking about our power coming in, and she mentioned something offhand about the most powerful act of persuasion was to plant ideas that would lead to what you wanted, rather than ordering someone to do it outright.

I tried to remember that as I continued to work my power on Julian.

It was working. I could tell by the way his eyes were slightly dazed looking. He was gaping at me like he would do anything for me, give me the world if he could.

"You should get the book right now," I told him soothingly. "Make sure that your alliance with the warden remains strong."

He nodded slowly and then pulled out his phone. "Bring the book to the prison. Now," he ordered to someone before hanging up and continuing to stare at me deliriously.

For a second, I was tempted to try and plant an idea to free the sirens. But I knew it wouldn't work. An act like that would dismantle too much of vampire society. He'd be met with so much opposition that even if my power were to last outside of me standing in his presence, which I doubted it would since I was inexperienced, the sirens would never be released.

While we waited for whoever he called to come to the prison with the book, I continued to tell him how good of an idea this was, how powerful he would be with the help of the warden, how he should always keep his commitments with him.

It was exasperating work, but I tried to think of it as a learning experience. Instead of thinking about what it would be like to have it ripped away, I would use this week to try and hone my skills, so that when I did get my power back, I wouldn't be like a newly born foal stumbling around with no clue how to use it.

And I would get my power back. If there was one thing this experience reinforced was that I could not live like half a person forever. I'd been motivated to get my power before, but then I'd gotten distracted. With Keon, Alaric, and Seth. I wouldn't forget the end goal this time.

My heart broke, thinking of all the sirens who lived permanently without their real self.

I wouldn't be like them. I couldn't.

The door suddenly opened, and the warden strode in, a big grin across his handsome albeit terrifying face. He was holding what looked like a thick gold-plated book under his arm, and he slow-clapped as he entered the room.

Whatever magic he contained in that clap dissipated all the hard work I'd just done on Julian. Julian's gaze became sharp and focused once more. He looked around the room as if he wondered how he'd gotten there.

His eyes flicked to me and then to the warden. I knew when he noticed the book because his entire being stiffened, a dangerous aura surrounding him.

"How did you get that?" he growled, right before a wave of recognition hit him. He turned towards me, and I knew that he saw me. He saw the cloak of power I held.

"That was a stupid thing for you to do, you little bitch," he seethed at me. He lunged at me, and my power cracked at him like it had with the warden, sudden and uncontrolled. Except unlike with the warden, my power struck home. A giant red welt appeared across Julian's face, and he yelped at the pain.

He lunged at me again, and again, my power struck, this time slicing him right across the neck. Julian's pallor had turned a furious purple color, a mix of embarrassment and rage I supposed.

I'd only seen him turn that color once before, the day I told him I'd given myself away to a stranger.

Julian would have killed me in that moment if he could have, but the warden stepped in right before he could lunge again.

"That's enough," he barked, but there was no real heat in his voice, only amusement. "You should have known better, Julian. Nobody double crosses me."

The words were more than a slap in Julian's face, they seemed like a warning as well. To me.

"You're both going to pay for this," Julian said in a

voice that was so enraged, he could barely get the words out.

He flew past both of us, vibrating with irritation and the promise of retribution. The door slammed behind him, and silence filled the room.

My body was beginning to tire. Controlling my power, or even wielding it, since it was obvious that I had very little control, was tiring, that was for sure.

I looked over at the warden, but he wasn't paying me any attention. He had the book open, and he was attentively going through it. The gold pages made a soft ringing sound as he flipped them. I gazed in amazement at the aura I could see around them. Whatever was contained in those pages was powerful.

No wonder Julian hadn't wanted to give it up.

I waited a few long moments before I cleared my throat. I was ready to get back to my cell, and it was almost time to start delivering meals. I was excited about the prospect of having a week to try out my powers. Maybe I could use them on the guys…make them do embarrassing crap or something.

"Selena, you did good work today," the warden said, that annoying amusement still laced through his voice.

"I did," I told him calmly, because my mother had once told me that a lady deflects compliments, and when I'd woken up from the dead, I was more determined than ever to be the opposite of her.

"I hope that was fun for you," he continued, and a trickle of unease began to build up inside of me…along with panic.

"It was good," I told him hesitantly.

"But I'm afraid that your fun is going to have to come to an end."

I just gaped at him. It took me a minute to understand what he was talking about.

"But you said a week," I told him softly. "I did everything you wanted."

He slowly closed the gold book and nodded in agreement. "You did do everything that I wanted. But you can't honestly believe that I could allow a prisoner with your kind of power to run amok among my prison, now could you?"

"This was all about Julian not keeping his word. You're doing that very same thing right now," I told him, trying to keep back the frustrated tears.

"I am, aren't I?" he said unrepentantly as he began to walk towards me.

I stood there shocked for a moment before my brain and my power woke up. It lashed out at him, and this time, I was helping it. Snap after snap sounded out in the room as my power struck at him.

But the warden just laughed as he swatted the bursts of power away like they were nothing but flies and continued to walk towards me.

I finally gave up, my chest heaving, once he was standing directly in front of me.

"You might have felt powerful up against someone like Julian, but he's nothing compared to me, little girl," the warden said in a soft voice that was more menacing than if he were screaming at me. "You're nothing when you walk these halls. I own you. I own every single prisoner in every single cell. And the fact that you haven't gotten that through your fucking head…well, you're more naïve than I thought. The idea that you would ever have a chance against me, you're out of your fucking mind."

He suddenly grasped both sides of my head, pulling on my hair until I grunted in pain and a tear slid down my face. He eyed the tear with interest before he began muttering something.

And then I felt it—my power being stripped away. It was like pieces of my soul were being hacked off with a jagged knife, and I screamed at the pain and the sensation of losing myself. Whatever the warden was doing, it was way more painful than it had been before.

When it was done, seemingly hours later, I collapsed to the ground, spent and weak, feeling like my entire world had imploded around me.

"Remember this lesson, little siren. I own you. That won't change until you're outside the walls of this place. And we both know that might never happen."

I lay there on the ground, staring at the wall as his footsteps faded away. It felt like all the hope had been sucked out of me, along with my energy…along with my power.

The door to the room opened and closed, and I was alone. I knew the guard would be in here soon, the warden wouldn't allow me time alone for long. So the second the heavy door slammed behind him, I let myself cry.

Life was indescribably hard sometimes.

With my power, something inside of me had filled up, become whole. I didn't need anyone else, or at least that's what it felt like for a couple of hours today.

But without my power, I was not only incomplete inside, I was also devastatingly reminded how alone I was.

The tears came hard and fast.

Just as I predicted, a guard arrived not two minutes later.

"Get up," he barked. It was the same guard as this morning. His voice wasn't as gruff as it had been though. Maybe he felt sorry for me.

I stumbled to my knees, feeling drunk and disoriented. My power made me so focused, so strong. I felt like I was just learning to walk as I struggled to stand, and eventually, the guard had to grab me in order for me to make it out of the room.

The walk to my cell seemed to be much longer than normal. My body was in physical pain. I was like an addict who needed her fix.

Keon appeared seemingly out of nowhere as we walked. He gave the guard a loaded look, and the guard practically threw me towards him as he all but ran away.

"Come here, baby," Keon whispered as he scooped me up in his arms.

Distraught, I couldn't be held accountable for my actions as I laid my head against his chest and wept.

"Whatever it is, I'll make it okay," he told me softly.

I shook against him, my sobs turning into manic laughs. I sounded crazy. And maybe I was. Maybe this had been the thing to push me over the edge.

The idea that this serial killer I'd found myself involved with could make everything better suddenly sounded like the most ridiculous thing I'd ever heard.

Keon didn't say anything, he just continued to walk to my cell, stroking my hair soothingly.

He opened up my cell and gently laid me down.

"Just go away, Keon," I told him as tears continued to flood out of my eyes.

"I'll make this right," he responded sadly, something that looked a lot like love in his eyes.

I didn't say anything in response.

After a long moment, where I could feel the weight of his gaze caressing my skin, he walked away.

The cell door clanged softly behind him.

Someday, everyone was going to pay.

I was going to get my power back. And when I did, I'd figure out a way for no one to ever take it again.

CHAPTER 6

SELENA

I curled in on myself in bed, the tears falling for so many reasons—for always being controlled, for being used by everyone, for feeling so helpless. I sobbed into the pillow, wanting everyone to hurt for doing that to me.

The warden was a cruel, cruel monster. Returning my power for such a short time was worse than not having it. To be teased with what should be mine, to finally feel like a complete person, only to have it ripped away broke me.

The memories of the warden's gloating words were sharp like razors, sinking into me like fangs.

All my life, I had been a survivor. A lost siren. Afraid.

In here, I'd changed and come so far, except that brutal experience with Julian and the warden at my expense took me full circle and back to that weak girl who'd first been tossed into Nightmare Penitentiary. I kept wiping the tears from my cheeks, but it made no difference, as more kept falling.

Somewhere in the distance, someone shouted, then laughed. There came heavy footfalls. Voices. More shouting. Just another day in this place, while I lay in my prison cell, my nerves gnawing until they were raw. On the inside, my soul was dying.

"ARE you just going to stand there and daydream?" Boris shouted from across the kitchen, eliciting laughter from the sink girls washing the trays. I'd come in early today for my first day back at delivering meals. My eyes felt puffy from crying most of yesterday, still feeling like fragments not yet put together.

Raising my head to meet his glare, an urgency ran through me to do my job and return things to as normal as possible. Last thing I wanted was to lose my job, no matter how mundane it was. It kept my body and mind busy.

Without wasting a beat, I hurried to collect the trays filled with food and stacked them onto the two shelves of my cart, and more on top.

Trevor waited at the door, opening it as I pushed the cart through and into the mess hall. Head down, I moved on with my job, a task that day in and day out, started to blend into one another. With no natural light in here, not being able to tell what time of the day it was made the whole day one large blur. I craved sunlight on my skin, and I kept remembering the fenced in courtyard where Alaric fought that snake shifter. It had been overcast, but anything was better than being in here.

That would be perfect, if I wasn't trying to avoid bumping into three men. Let alone any other freak in the place who got their backs up if I walked past their prison cell. The whole place was like a gang war zone, sections run by different factions. The more I delivered meals, the more I observed and started to understand the mechanics of the penitentiary.

There were multiple levels of hierarchy, each with their own leader or alpha. Hell, there were so many alpha males in this place, I was surprised they hadn't killed each other yet. Somehow, the whole lot of them had worked out some kind of truce. Each staying in their own sector seemed to do the trick. And that meant I stayed out of those jurisdictions.

"You're quiet," Trevor said out of the blue as we headed down the long, dimly lit corridor that led us toward the underground bridge to maximum security.

I glanced over to him, the guy had short dark hair and a crooked nose. "I rarely talk on our deliveries."

He nodded, not appearing to really be listening to me by the way he stared right through me. "So I heard you died. Rumors are spreading like wildfire."

I blinked at him several times, my mind racing to understand his real purpose for asking this question, and after dealing with the warden, I had no intention of feeding the beast. "I don't want to talk about it." I kept pushing my cart. The wheels squeaked each time they hit a bumpy surface on the stone floor, echoing against the walls.

The notion still sat heavily on my thoughts. To come back from the dead wasn't a picnic in the park. What if I didn't come back completely right? And why the hell did I still hear that ringing in my ear? I felt so out of sorts still, so I knew in my bones that something was wrong. I just wasn't sure how to find out. Not like I could walk up to the penitentiary doctor and explain that something felt broken inside me. And especially not with the way Trevor was sniffing around for information. That told me the warden was curious, and that was dangerous.

"My grandpa died," Trevor said, strolling alongside me.

"Oh, I'm so sorry," I answered, looking up at him as he studied the path in front of us.

"He's not dead anymore. The doctors brought him back on the operating table, but they say he was gone for a whole seven minutes. And you know what he said?"

"What's that?" He had me curious, especially since I didn't seem to remember anything from my afterlife experience.

"In the afterlife, he met a woman in a waiting room, and she told him it wasn't his time and that he had fourteen years."

My mouth dropped open. "Years left to live?"

He shrugged. "We all think so. That's four years

away now, and I've been trying to research everything in the afterlife to find a way to make sure he doesn't die in four years. So I've been speaking to people who've had near death experiences to see what they saw."

The way he looked at me, with a pleading expression, might have melted my resolve if I had something to tell him. "Wish I could help."

His jaw tightened, and we traveled the rest of the way in silence, while I chewed on what Trevor had said. I had no plans on asking him more questions, but it did remind me to head into the library for research later. With the kitchen keeping me busy most of the day, either preparing trays or delivering them, I ran out of time to do much else. Well, at least during library hours.

The shift went quicker than I expected. I'd done several trips back and forth with additional meals into the maximum-security sector. Head down, ignoring the inmates' comments, I just delivered food and kept going. My mind raced with everything of late and what exactly I'd do about it.

Dying.

Betrayal.

Alaric's insistence I was his. And I had no doubt Keon would be the same, and not to mention Seth. Laz came to mind too. Had I just made things a hundred times more complicated by sleeping with him?

Our footfalls echoed in the quiet corridor, my ears still buzzing with the humming sound that refused to abide.

As we merged back into the main part of the prison, having passed security gates and checkpoints, the rousing noise of voices climbed. We turned into the main thoroughfare that connected the main hall with prison cells that seemed to stretch out endlessly. The mess hall lay in this direction too.

Unease curled in my stomach at being here, knowing that people talked about me, that I had guys watching my every move. I wanted nothing more than to vanish.

The growing list of events in my life wore on me, but I refused to let it get me down.

An explosive scream shattered the normal prison sounds from somewhere behind us. I flinched around as a silence fell over the place, most people turning in the same direction.

The scream came again, and a sudden flurry of guards rushed right past us. Everyone parted for them, and I peered down the same direction, curious about what just happened.

Murmured words came from behind me, and I glanced over my shoulder to Trevor pressing his ear piece, nodding. Next thing, his face blanched and looked at me. "Return the cart to the kitchen quickly on your own. I have to go."

"What happened?" I asked, but he rushed right past me, completely ignoring me.

My skin crawled at what could have scared him and drawn the other guards. Hastily, I grabbed the cart and wove my way back to the kitchen. Once I returned it and washed the trays, I made my way to the library, noting it should be open another hour or so.

A strange eeriness had fallen over the prison, and the hairs on my arms rose in response. I moved faster down the hallways, people too distracted to pay me any attention, and soon enough, I stood outside the grand doors leading into the library, and they were spread open.

I stepped inside, the smell of musty books filling me, and I breathed easy. There was a calmness in here that helped with the buzzing in my head, with still not feeling like myself in my own body. I couldn't shake off the sensation that I was a stranger in my head.

Just as I'd done while I was growing up, I threw myself into books to escape reality. The smell alone calmed me. Rows of shelves filled the space in the second half of the room, while the first part had long tables and benches, not too dissimilar to the ones in the mess hall. There were only five other people in there from what I could see, and maybe this was a place I'd visit more frequently. I didn't see anyone following me in here.

Using the small computer for searching books, I typed in "afterlife."

Numerous searches popped up, many titles about dying and religious texts, but it was a good place to start. I took note of the row and number of one book, and made my way down a row. Then I went to town and started searching.

It didn't take long before I ended up with a high pile

of books in front of me as I sat at one of the tables and began scanning each one for anything that talked about coming back from the dead.

Nothing.

That's what I found, and I sighed, leaning back in my chair.

"Wouldn't you love to use Google right now?" A deep voice came from behind me. Someone I recognized, and I straightened in my seat as he slid in across the table from me.

"Do you have a way for me to access Google, or are you just teasing?"

Laz grabbed the top book, titled *Coming Back*, and flipped through the book. "Sweet cakes, there's only one way I'm going to tease you, and that involves stripping you down." He glanced up, a wicked grin pulling at his mouth. Then he shut the book with a clapping sound and dumped it on the table. "Trying to find out about death after your encounter?"

In all honesty, I didn't know if he was aware that I had died or had just listened to the rumors. I shrugged. "I'm curious, but these books are crap. Either religious or scientific explanations and not what I want."

He shifted forward, his arms leaning on the table. "Hate to break it to you, but no one really knows what happens after death until they're too far gone from this plane of existence. Now, how about we head back to my room? I can think of other ways to make you float on clouds." The way he so easily slipped that into his sentence about death told me he had no problems with picking up women.

For a moment, I visualized myself under him, his strong body caging me in as he rammed into me. A delicious shiver raced down to the pit of my stomach at the memory of us together. Except, he was a distraction, and I refused to let him affect me beyond that.

I stood up, my seat pushed backward, sliding over the wooden floorboards. "Well, it's been nice chatting with you." I grabbed the bundle of books to return them.

"But—"

"No, Laz. I meant what I said before. If we're going to chat, then it's just that. Nothing else. It was a one-off thing."

I expected him to protest or pout, but instead, he got to his feet and came over to me. "I can respect that." He collected the books from my arms. "But I'm also a man who never gives up on what I want. And you are in my sights." He turned away before I could respond and strolled to the rows of shelves to return my books. My gaze slipped down to the way he wore his orange jumpsuit rolled down to his waist, the black tee pulled tight across his muscles that shifted across his back.

Who the heck was this guy?

I let out a long breath and rushed out of the library before I did exactly what I promised myself I wouldn't.

Ten seconds later, I marched down the corridor away from the library and made my way to my prison cell. I felt stares on me, so I tried to make myself as small as possible and get out of the main thoroughfare. Something drew my attention to the next level up, and leaning against the railing was Keon.

Watching me.

Eyes locked on me.

I pressed my lips together, hating how tense he made me, how when I looked at him, I couldn't forget the possessiveness of his kisses. Or that the monster living inside him had killed me.

My stomach knotted, and I half expected him to come down after me, but he never made a move. There was no way I could escape him, was there? Still, the torturous tug-of-war of emotions inside me continued. How did I balance the remorse I knew he felt at what he'd done with the danger he put me in?

I marched forward, putting distance between us before I backed down, making the decision that running away from him or Alaric or Seth wasn't going to work. They would make sure of that, and with how much I craved them...well, I had to change my approach.

A solution slipped into my mind. One of retribution. The thing about these men wasn't that they hated me. Quite the opposite. It all came down to me being their possession, their object to use as it favored them, not always me.

I'd keep emotions out of this, and make it a pure lesson for them to understand what it felt like to be used. I'd uncover their strengths and weaknesses, what each truly wanted, then I'd rip it away. Couldn't be that hard to find out. They loved bragging about themselves.

I glanced over my shoulder to Keon, still up on the next floor up, staring my way. My lips quirked into a tight grin, and I walked away, murmuring under my breath, "You won't even see me coming."

CHAPTER 7

KEON

It has been two days since I'd last spoken with Selena. I'd given her space, exactly what she wanted. But I'd kept myself busy with the recent outbreak of fights between two of the clans in here. The felines had declared war against the snake shifters, so most days had ended up in bloody warfare. Now, the lot of them were locked up in solitary confinement to cool the fuck down. Who the hell knew what sparked that off, but it didn't take much, seeing as everyone was bored as shit.

I sighed and walked the halls for my shift, strolling right past a fight. Selena was getting to me, dammit. Not even watching others brutally beat each other up brought me joy any longer. I obsessed about her day and night, and I doubted I'd be staying away from her for much longer. I had to make her understand, and that meant sharing what lived inside me. Something I'd never told a soul about.

Someone from the fight screamed.

"For fuck's sake."

I swung toward them and shoved others aside, instantly recognizing the guy on the floor getting beaten. A smart-mouthed prick who I was surprised wasn't dead yet. I snatched one asshole on top of him by the scruff of his neck and hurled him backward. He crashed into the bystanders, causing a larger racket. Hope they beat him up.

Then I turned to the skinnier guy, snatched his shirt, and heaved him to his feet. In his face, I spat, "Don't start fights you can't finish. Now get the fuck out of my face."

He took off hastily, and I turned to the crowd. "Nothing to see. Get back to whatever you were doing." Slowly, they disbanded, including the guy I tossed aside. There was definitely a benefit to extra strength when working in a place like this.

I kept moving on my rounds, when a cheering sound came from the direction of the mess hall. What was in the water today? I rounded the corner to reach the end of this corridor. Doors stood wide open, and inside, the masses congregated around the tables. And up on them, stood two people facing each other.

My stomach dropped the second I recognized one of them as Selena.

The fuck!

Her brow furrowed, and she turned toward the brunette twice her size, her lips moving, but I couldn't make out the words beyond the explosion of hoots.

Had she been forced into a fight? I darted forward, just as she lunged at her opponent. Ducking low, she rammed her shoulder into the brunette with such strength, the girl bent over from the pain. But not before she drove a fist into Selena's back.

I cringed, pushing people out of my way who were rushing to the mess hall. Legs pumping, my boots smacked the floor, and I wove myself closer.

Another guard stood just inside the room, leaning against the door, arms crossed, watching the spectacle, grinning. That would be me, except my girl was up there.

Suddenly, she unleashed a war cry and threw herself at the brunette, fists swinging. She was feral, and received her own fair share of hits. A thrill raced through me at seeing my little warrior, and damn, I was proud of her, but after what she just went through, she shouldn't be fighting. And most importantly, since when did she behave this way?

My heart spun with confusion. The feisty girl up on the table wasn't behaving like Selena.

"Out of my way," I growled, carving a path through the crowd. Reaching the table, I snatched Selena's pants and tugged her in my direction, just as she ducked a swinging punch.

Losing her balance, her arms jutted out, cart-wheeling as she fell.

I caught her in my arms and held her cradled as she shoved her fists against my chest.

"Put me down," she cried as the crowd booed me, and her opponent stood over us.

Fury bled through my veins. I jerked my head up to meet her gaze. "Get the fuck down before I get up there and you'll end up in the infirmary for a month straight." I didn't hurt women or children. Even I held onto a code I followed, but if she hurt my Selena, I was going in blazing.

"I will finish her," Selena roared, wriggling in my arms, and I grasped her tighter.

The brunette's lips pinched, defeat flaring over her face. She turned and hopped off the table before blending in with the masses. Their whispers flooded the room. I lowered Selena to her feet and grasped her wrist as she flung herself after the girl.

Dragging her to my side, I hissed, "What the fuck is going on? Did she hurt you?"

She sucked in a long breath, her nostrils flaring as she looked up at me. Something swam behind her eyes, and for those few moments, she stared at me like she didn't recognize me.

"Are you all right?" I asked. A chill seeped into my gut and spread outward.

"Yeah of course. But you shouldn't have stopped me. I was winning."

I licked my dried lips, pulling back the anger rising through me. "You're coming with me." Not waiting for her to respond, I hauled her out of the mess hall to the amusement of the other inmates, who cheered. Fucking asses.

"Keon, stop." She wrenched against my grip as I dragged her down the corridor. She punched my hand, and I swung back around and came face to face with her. Inches away, she didn't back down, and there was something fucking sexy about a woman who stood toe to toe against me.

"What's gotten into you? Since when do you fight other inmates? If you want to give the warden any reason to dismiss you from your delivery work, you're doing a great job." I couldn't believe I, of all people, was trying to talk sense into her.

Her nose wrinkled. "What do you care? You tried to kill me, remember?" Her eyes shone, lips stretching wide.

Who the hell was she today? "Selena," I warned, the word hissing through my clenched teeth.

"I want out of here." Raising her chin to me, she hurled her fist, whacking me right in the jaw. I saw it coming but didn't react, purely out of shock, and her small bony hand carried a sharp bite. Grinding my teeth, I squeezed my grip on her wrist until she grimaced.

"Nothing good can come out of this for you," I reprimanded her.

"Is that right, lover boy? How about you let your demon out again and let's fight."

What the fuck?

She didn't back down, but I wasn't having this conversation in front of everyone.

"Move," I yelled in an inmate's face for standing

close to us, watching us, then I marched, still gripping her wrist. We made our way back down the hallway and along another passage until we reached her prison cell. She stumbled inside and glanced around, then back at me. The flash of darkness in her eyes unnerved me. I'd never seen her this way, and it worried me that the shock of what I'd done to her had pushed her over the edge of sanity.

"What do you want?" she asked, fierceness behind her voice. "To fuck me to make yourself feel better for what you did?"

My throat tightened. "I get you're pissed at me, and I want to explain everything."

She turned away and flopped onto the bed, disinterested.

"But this isn't the right time," I conceded, studying her as she lay down, her head nestled on the pillow. Seconds later, her deep breaths told me she slept.

"Selena?" I stepped closer and stared down at her lost to dream world. Crouching in front of her, I pushed loose strands off her brow. "What is going on with you? One minute, you're jumping off the walls, then you're asleep?"

Her response came in the form of rolling over and curling in on herself as her breathing deepened.

I clenched my hands. How badly had I goddamn broken her? My beast gave a small growl from the pit of my gut that whatever she was going through was my fault. Of course it was. Pieces of me slipped apart at what I did to her.

My heart shattered at seeing her teetering on the edge of falling apart. I'd have to arrange for her to meet with the doc and find out what was going on.

I got up and walked out to let her sleep in peace. I checked my watch. Only a few more hours until my shift ended, and I just wasn't sure if I was ready to leave, knowing Selena struggled.

Selena

MY EYES FLUTTERED open to the ringing sound of the morning bell that announced breakfast was being served. It took me seconds to ground myself as I searched my mind for the last thing I remembered and how it could be morning already.

I'd delivered food into max security with Trevor then returned to my cell. Then my thoughts were a blur. I must have been so exhausted that I crashed and slept half a day and all night.

Rubbing my eyes, I pushed my legs out of bed when a shocking shot of pain raced up my back.

"Ouch." I stretched to ease the ache when I spotted a huge purple bruise on my arm, like someone had punched me. "What in the world?" I ran a thumb over the sore spot, wondering if I'd bumped myself into something during delivery.

Then I remembered breakfast time meant I was

on shift. "Oh, fuck! Boris is going to freak." I threw myself up, rushed to the toilet in my room, swiped on deodorant, and ripped off yesterday's jumpsuit. In record time, I was dressed in orange pants and a black short sleeved tee. Stepping into my boots, I then ran out of my prison cell and toward the mess hall.

The crowds heading in for a meal were relentless and blocking up my way, while my heart hammered in my chest that I'd be fired. It wasn't the best job, but it sure beat sitting around doing nothing, plus I enjoyed getting to see more of the penitentiary and understanding how it worked.

It felt like forever until I finally burst into the mess hall. Tables were crammed with inmates, and the line for food was halfway along the wall. Guards were posted at every end, but none were Keon. I wasn't ready to talk to him yet since the whole being killed and all.

The smell of scrambled eggs and toast filled the air, and I frantically wove past people to reach the back door. I knocked on it loudly when one of the girls serving at the counter over to my right glanced over. Mary was the nicest worker, and she quickly ducked into the back. Seconds later, the door unlocked and opened.

"Thanks."

"He's pissed," she said, and my stomach dropped instantly.

I hurried inside and locked the door as Mary

returned to her station with impatient inmates demanding food.

The kitchen was abuzz with four cooks, another two washing the trays of finished food coming in.

Boris sat in the corner at his small table, scribbling something in a folder. My nerves were on edge, but I made quick haste over to him.

His head lifted, eyes meeting mine, and his brow furrowed into a dozen lines. "If you can't meet the time of your shift, I don't need you," he barked so everyone in the kitchen heard. And I had no doubt they all listened.

I cringed but stood tall, refusing to let him get to me. I freaking died, and all they gave me was one day leeway. "I promise, it won't happen again," I said, biting the real words I wanted to say about him being a selfish asshole who didn't care about anyone but looking good in front of the warden.

He stared at me, not saying a word. "Get out of my face. Tomorrow, you're on lunch duty. Be on time or don't bother returning."

I nodded and started to retreat. "Thank you."

Without wasting a moment, I headed out just as Mary approached me with a tray of food. "Here you go," she whispered. "He's really foul today, so count yourself lucky to not be working." She grinned, and I could have hugged her for her kindness. Sometimes, a few words and a sweet gesture was all it took to make things better.

"You're the best. Thank you."

She hurried back to work, and I headed out into the mess hall with my tray. Just then, four people left their table at one end, and I hurried to claim one seat for myself. If I wasn't working this morning, then I might spend it doing more research in the library.

I started eating the baked beans and scrambled egg, then buttered my toast. The flavors still sparked on my tongue, but not as flavorsome as they had a few days ago. I frowned, but it didn't deter me from eating.

Someone sat in front of me. In fact, it was two women, both looking older, with silvering hair, but the age lines on their faces spoke of hardship. A spark of yellow flared in their eyes. Witches. I had no idea the prison had any in here, though not that it mattered, seeing as so many of the inmates' abilities were muted. And I assumed the warden would not allow magic wielding inmates to walk around freely in his prison.

I smiled, then when they frowned, I regretted it.

"Bitch, you stole my dreamcatcher," the woman with short cropped hair accused. "I let it go when you took my bag of herbs. Almost felt sorry for you, but I was wrong, wasn't I, thief?"

I glanced behind me at first, convinced she must be referring to someone else. "Are you talking to me?" I asked, completely perplexed.

She shoved my tray of food off the table, and it hit the floor, the last bit of toast I hadn't eaten now butter face down, and I sighed.

"I was going to eat that," I snapped.

"No one cares about your stupid toast," she

snapped. "I want my dreamcatcher back," she sneered, while her friend watched me like she might leap over the table any second to strangle me.

"Look, I don't even know what you're talking about. Why would I take your stuff? I don't even know where your cell is."

Her friend slammed a hand to the table, her upper lip curling upward. "Stop lying. Why the fuck did you take her stuff?"

A small crowd clustered near us now, and the whole mess hall had fallen silent, staring our way.

A shiver raced up my spine.

"We saw you, bitch!" the short-haired woman snarled. "Now you can come clean and return my stuff, or I'm painting this table with your blood."

A hooting cheer roused around us from everyone else wanting a fight.

I flinched at how quickly this was getting out of hand, and I had no clue what I was being accused of. "We can go check in my cell, and you'll see I don't have anything of yours. Maybe you saw someone who looked like me? I don't know what to tell you."

The women exchanged looks, the main one stating, "Looks like she's not going to come clean." They glanced my way, and my blood turned to ice. I wasn't a fighter, but I wouldn't sit back either. Except, I stood no chance against two of them.

I got up slowly, figuring my only chance to avoid a full out brawl meant heading back into the kitchen. And this was why I had to stop eating my meals in the mess hall. No one ever left me the hell alone. "Let's talk about this. Whatever you are missing, I'm sure I can help you find it."

"Fight, fight, fight," some guy bellowed.

I cringed on the inside.

The witches were up on their feet, the short haired one pushing her sleeves up to her elbows.

I curled my hands into fists, ready to give as much as it took if I couldn't get away quick enough. Heat rushed to my face and spread across my chest.

A sudden boom of laughter rocked me on the spot and had the two crazy women turning toward the crowd.

Alaric shoved past the masses and emerged, clapping, his eyes on the women. "Wonderful. Exactly what we needed over our boring lunch. Witch drama. Now, why don't you two broomstick worshippers get the fuck out of here before I show you exactly where to stick your magic."

I wouldn't deny that he couldn't have arrived at a better time. Sure, I should hate that he came to my rescue in front of everyone, but fuck them. I didn't owe them anything, and most loathed me anyway, so who gave a shit. In fact, it was better they all thought Alaric was my guard as they might leave me the hell alone.

The witches stood their ground, glaring at him, and the crowd pressed in, anticipating and most likely hoping for a fight.

A softness stroked down my arms, something invisible and so faint, it had me glancing down to see if someone touched me. With it came a burning warmth that swept over my chest, sliding deeper to the pit of my stomach. Heat coiled between my legs, and I shot my head up toward Alaric, the desire for him rising in me like a metal spring wound so tight, I might burst if I didn't unleash it.

The witches blinked at him, suddenly doe-eyed and gushing over him, touching his arms, flirting.

I rolled my eyes, while a spike of jealousy awoke within me. Except I knew this was his doing—he was using his incubus power to get the women to back off. And well, it worked too well, because they looked ready to undress.

Not to mention the other women in the room pushing forward to get a piece of him.

The sexy demon leaned toward the witches. "How does it feel?" His voice was pure lust, and a shudder shot through me at hearing him. I stepped forward instinctively.

The short haired witch gasped, her hand reaching to her breast, and she squeezed.

Then just as quick, the heated sensation vanished as though someone had tossed a bucket of icy water over me.

That time, I gasped out loud, and the rest of the women around us stumbled on their feet, taken aback by how their intense desires had just been ripped away.

Breathing heavily, the witches looked at each other and then back at Alaric, hatred spewing from their gazes. "You fucking bastard."

"You so much as look at my girl again, and I can tease you until it drives you to madness. How does that sound?"

He could do that? The shock on their faces was palpable, and I didn't blame them. The sensation that just rocked through me was the most intense build up to an orgasm I'd experienced without even being touched. I shouldn't be excited that he told them I was his girl or that I'd experienced him firsthand and it was better than any of these women could ever imagine.

He wasn't someone I could trust, I reminded myself, though I also found it sweet that he came to my rescue the way he had. I was a walking contradiction, my emotions all over the place.

When Alaric turned toward me, it took me several tries to find my voice. Currently, it was stuck in the realm of arousal, still unable to believe the ferociousness of his power.

"Let's get out of here," he told me, then took hold of my hand and guided me out of the mess hall.

Protesting was out of the question, considering he saved my ass and I wasn't about to look a gift horse in the mouth.

"What was that all about?" he asked me, still grasping my arm and dragging me down a quiet corridor, then another. I forgot how many we turned down, and I didn't remember this part of the penitentiary. Except that meant nothing in a place that was alive and moved, revealing new passages all the time.

I shrugged. "They were both delusional, that's what.

I don't know what they were talking about. As if I'd steal their stuff. What would I want with a dream-catcher?"

"Sounds to me like they were just looking for a reason to hurt you."

"Why?" I asked, cutting him a long stare. "You heard something?"

He laughed, and while he sounded like the most delicious thing when he made that sound, a flare of anger also rolled over me. "Hey, don't patronize me." I ripped my arm from his grip.

"Sorry, gorgeous, it's just that in here, no one needs an excuse to start up a fight. It could be that they woke up on the wrong side of the bed, they were bored, someone beat them up. Who the fuck knows? But they were just preying on you."

"Maybe," I answered, unsure. The witches seemed so specific in what they accused me of. And I'd never laid eyes on them before, so how would they know me? And what in the world would I want with their witchy things?

Movement caught my attention to the couple walking right past us, staring our way, then vanished around a corner.

"I know where we can go and be alone," he suggested.

My knee-jerk reaction was to reject him and walk away, but then I remembered my plan was to make them think I had forgiven them, to gather information about them I could use later. Of course it sucked that he'd just saved me, but that didn't change anything. He'd lied and used me, so I looked up at him and smiled. "I'd like that."

He didn't respond at first, clearly surprised by how easily I gave in. I cursed myself for being so obvious, because in truth, it was so much easier to give in to him than push him away. Maybe this was going to be harder than I anticipated.

Taking a deep breath, I said, "Are we going to just stand here and stare at each other?"

He nodded, and his curious expression cracked with a hint of a smirk. "This way."

Before long, we were going down stairs, then back up another set, the scenery the same—stone walls and dimly lit corridors.

"Do you know where you're going?" I asked, gaining myself a mischievous grin. "Or is your plan to make sure I don't remember my way back? Fooled you, because I've been keeping an eye on all the turns we took," I lied but wanted to see his reaction, which came in the form of him chuckling to himself.

I wasn't sure how to take that, but I didn't overthink it. If I let myself go there, I'd have found thousands of reasons to turn around and head back to the main prison sector.

"Do I scare you?" he asked over his shoulder.

"Really? That's what you think?" I fake laughed.

He shrugged nonchalantly.

"Of course not, but it does feel like you are taking me somewhere far away."

"You lack trust," he told me bluntly. Then he paused in front of a wall and set his palm flat against it. He mumbled something under his breath. Next thing, the wall shifted right before my eyes, and the stone evaporated as a black door came forward.

"Whoa, how did you do that?" I stepped forward as he pushed the door open.

He waved me inside, and I entered a large room with no windows, but it had lights overhead. There was a leather couch sitting in front of a large screen television on the wall. In the other corner sat a small counter with drawers and a small fridge.

"What is this room?" I wasn't sure where to look first but naturally drifted over and flopped down on the couch.

"It's a secret I created with a lot of magic I borrowed from others in the prison for favors."

"What sort of favors?" I glanced over the back of the couch at him as he shut the door and wandered over to the make-shift kitchen.

"Mostly stuff from outside these walls. You'd be surprised how much some people will pay for chocolate. Anyway, it's my small room away from everything when I need to escape."

"If I had this room, I'd stay here all the time."

"Well, it's a secret room for a purpose, and if I want to keep it, I can't let the guards find out."

I nodded and slid back into the soft embrace of the couch, suddenly feeling more comfortable than I had in too long. My bed was lumpy and hard. It seemed I'd forgotten what comfort felt like.

Alaric returned, handed me a can of coke and tossed me a bar of chocolate.

I caught it with one hand as my mouth fell open. "Are you kidding me?" Not waiting for a response, I ripped the packet and bit right into the block. Velvety sweet heaven danced on my tongue, and I almost wanted to cry at how badly I had missed this.

Alaric just stared at me, and I gripped the chocolate tighter. "Oh, did you want some?" I took another quick bite.

He chuckled as he sat on the other end of the couch. "It's all yours, pet. I'm worried I might get my fingers bitten off if I get too close."

"Seriously, I have never been happier to see chocolate." Two mouthfuls later, I set it down on the coffee table beside me and opened up my soda, then took a long sip. The sweetness flooded me, the best taste in the world.

"I'm glad I could bring you some joy. What you went through recently is horrific, and I am here for you, gorgeous. For anything."

Swallowing another mouthful of drink, I watched the way he pulled up a bent leg between us, how relaxed he looked. I reminded myself who I dealt with. An incubus. A warlord. A powerful man who was used to always getting his way. But it was still strange to have a normal conversation with this man who I'd had sex with and who melted my insides each time he so much as looked at me. I still remembered the first time he took me in the kitchen, the moment a savage explosion of arousal, heady and full of desperation. But I learned there was so much more to Alaric than maybe most realized in the penitentiary.

I set my drink down and turned to face him, leaning into the softness of the couch. It took every ounce of strength I had to not crawl over into his lap and taste his lips. Instead, I took a deep breath to calm myself.

He studied my face.

"What are you staring at?" I asked.

"Trying to read your expression. You've gone through so much trauma lately, and I'm worried about you." He reached over, his hand laying on top of mine in my lap. There was only tenderness, which was different to his usual possessiveness.

I tilted my head to the side. "And what do you see?"

"Someone brave. Someone hiding their fear. Someone so beautiful inside and out that it breaks me to know of your suffering."

A tinge of surprise struck me. That wasn't the response I expected, nor did I expect my body to tremble slightly at how close to the truth he skirted, except I had to keep reminding myself of who I dealt with. I saw him first hand with the warden, talking about the scepter after he'd grilled me about it.

"You're a real sweet talker, you know," I teased him. "But you don't owe me anything to hand out such compliments."

His fingers brushed across my arm, causing goosebumps to race up my skin, awakening a deep desire, a reminder of the pleasure he brought out in me. "But I do owe you. I should have been there when Keon went AWOL."

I frowned at his words. "What happened wasn't on you."

"I can't sleep at night, thinking about how badly things turned out."

He shuffled close across the couch, the side of his thigh touching my bent knee, and a smile flickered across his face. "Thanks for talking with me. For a while there, I feared you'd push me away as you had Keon."

Emotions welled inside me, squeezing my chest at his sincerity. I was dwarfed by his size, yet he stared at me with such affection. Was he truly moved by nearly losing me, or was this another game?

"When I was young, I almost died. Maybe I did die, no one really knows," he admitted.

I stiffened and eyed him with shock. "What happened?"

"My father had a horrible temper, and one day, I pushed him too far. He left me beaten so badly, I passed out. The servant who found me insisted I had been dead, but my father wouldn't hear a word of it. He is a real asshole."

I leaned in closer, torn to hear his father abused him so severely. "I'm so sorry." I placed my hand on his, and the earlier spark ignited through my veins like it always did in his presence. "Do you remember anything after passing out?"

"Stars."

I wrinkled my brow and pulled back. "Like stars in the sky?"

He shrugged. "They were all around me. So maybe. A psychic once told me death followed me, since I had crossed over at a young age."

His eyes lifted to mine, and with each passing second, the vulnerability painted on his face hardened back to the man who was always strong and unmoved. His story pained me, as it seemed it wasn't just me who grew up with terrible parents.

To change the topic, I asked, "How do you get away with so much in this place? This room for example. You told me before you had men who worked for you everywhere, but does that include the guards?"

"Where is this coming from?" He arched an eyebrow, his low intimidating tone ramping up my pulse.

But I wouldn't fall prey and overreact, so I shrugged. "Well, ever since my brush with death, I want to know who I'm dealing with so I don't get hurt again." Every word was the truth. "It's the new me."

"Oh, baby girl." He leaned in, cupping the side of my face, and his fingers swept through my hair to the back of my head. "I would destroy every last person in this place to keep you safe if you let me. I'd bring out their most dreaded fears and make them relive it over and over, not giving them reprieve. Not a single fucking second. They'd pay for ever laying a hand on you. Just say the word, and I'll take out Keon."

"No." My response shot out quickly.

"You like him a lot," he said, a thread of jealousy flaring over his face.

"He killed me, so no, I don't like him, but I don't want him dead. And I will deal with my own problems."

I should've pushed him away, instead I sat before him as his fingers slid down to the back of my neck to the soft flesh, where they pressed into my flesh to hold me in place. His presence swallowed me. The protectiveness he promised awakened a primal need to nestle against him, to accept his safety. Except was that what he was counting on? Was he preying on that part of me that would always fear the criminals in the penitentiary? Or was I overthinking it all?

I nearly caved and kissed him, nearly curled myself around him, nearly made him mine. Anything to ease the fiery ache between my thighs. Though, he seemed different today. Softer. Unguarded. Still, I held back my truth.

"You truly are amazing," he whispered.

I licked my lips, and his gaze fell to my mouth. In a sudden spark, the energy around us changed to something fiery, something electric. All I could think about was needing his touch all over my body. To let my body mold against his, to have him lavish me with kisses, greedily tear my clothes off. And then what? While I still retained some basic control over my lust, I pulled back and grabbed my drink, taking a few sips, then said, "You never answered my question."

He gave me a nod and pulled back, sitting tall next to me. "Ask me anything. I have nothing to hide."

The temptation to just ask about the scepter pressed on the forefront of my mind. Then wasn't I just falling prey to him once again, letting him know what truly plagued my mind? He was no fool and would know I wasn't revealing everything.

"You want to know about me. Yes, I have a handful of guards under my command. Several of the shifter packs in the penitentiary have also sworn me allegiance, all of them feeding me information. The warden has no clue he has spies under his own roof. Remember, I am here voluntarily to search for things that if I find will mean my territory outside will never be challenged again."

I recalled his explanation, so having that many connections, it made sense he'd get his way most of the time and that he always remained informed. Was that part of his play with the warden when I overheard them?

"Is Keon one of these guards?"

He chuckled. "Fuck no. That one's a dangerous wild card. The demon inside him is unpredictable as fuck, and let's just say, that wasn't the first time I've heard of Keon finishing a fight that way."

I pursed my lips. "He's killed someone before," I said matter-of-factly.

He nodded.

A shiver gripped my spine. "Why didn't anyone tell me about Keon?"

Alaric's lips pursed. "The real question is, why didn't he tell you himself?"

My heart twisted with the recollection of the day Keon attacked me, but I wouldn't allow myself to be swallowed by the darkness.

I watched Alaric's face change like he read my thoughts.

"How did you get into the business of being a warlord anyway?" I asked, drawing my knees up to my chest and hugging them, needing to change my thoughts about Keon before they consumed me.

"Family. I grew up with my father running his own territory. Well, until I took over at a very young age. Forced me to grow up quickly."

I wanted to find out secrets about him, weaknesses, but instead, I was left with my heart clenching at his hardship.

The silent pause stretched between us, until he said, "Want to watch a movie?"

"Sure," I replied. "Something funny please."

He laughed and got up to collect the remote from near the television. "Let me see what I can find for us."

Before long, we were both huddled close, his arm around my back and me leaning against his side, the lights out, and the start of the only movie available called *JoJo Rabbit*. Name sounded funny. We both cuddled like we were at the theater.

It was a strange sensation to feel torn between

desperately wanting to give myself over to Alaric and reminding myself constantly that he had been playing me. And more than anything, I wished we could just be together without any complications or deceit. But I worried I was making a bad, bad decision.

CHAPTER 8

SELENA

My eyes fluttered open to silence and an empty hallway. Panic squeezed my insides as I frantically looked around to find myself slumped against the wall while everyone else was locked up in their cell. It had to be the middle of the night by the stillness. I moved to get up when something sharp stabbed my palm. I flinched and looked down to a long black feather with a point at the end, pricking my hand. I tossed it aside.

The primal terror of feeling utterly lost crashed into me. I scrambled to my feet, catching sight of the prison cell I stood next to, the door sitting slightly ajar. Inside, the floor was covered in more black feathers. I scratched my neck, and my hand came back with another feather. My eyes widened as I desperately patted myself, only to find more of the little things all over me like I'd just plucked a chicken.

What was going on with me?

I scanned the rest of the room for what I'd done, finally spotting a taxidermic raven on the floor, completely plucked, its stiff body lying inches away from the back shelves.

I gasped and lifted my gaze to the bunk beds where the two witches from the mess hall were fast asleep. Ice filled my veins.

Slowly recoiling, I held my breath, too afraid to make a sound to wake them and find out what I'd done. What the fuck had I done? I thought they'd gone mad when they'd accused me of stealing their stuff. Except they were right. Oh God, I was losing my mind.

Fright gripped me. When I was far enough away from their room, I turned and ran toward my prison cell. The overhead lights cast a muted glow, my light footfalls hitting the floor. There was no one in sight.

The door to my room was open, and shock rattled through me. Had someone opened the doors on purpose, but why the witches? Shaking, I darted inside and dragged the door shut behind me. I had enough crap going on with me that I didn't need someone playing pranks on me. Or was this all me?

Last thing I remembered was Alaric walking me back to my room after I'd bawled my eyes out at the movie he picked. Who would put such a funny name on a story revolving around Hitler? By the time I started crying, I was too far invested to stop watching it. But I was left with a shredded heart. Alaric held me as I cried, which only added to my confused emotions, where I knew I had to push him away, but he felt so good at the same time.

And then after dinner, I had gone to sleep like most nights. Shaking, I hugged myself and searched the room for anything out of the ordinary. It all looked normal. So instead, I got undressed, plucked every damn feather I could find and flushed them down the toilet. Then I pulled on new clothes. A quick look in the small, warped mirror near the sink, and I plucked out three more feathers. I leaned close and stared into my eyes to see if anything appeared out of sorts. Aside from some redness from exhaustion, they seemed normal.

I hurried into my bed and ducked under the blankets, curling in on myself. What was wrong with me? I'd broken into someone's cell to pluck their dead raven?

My teeth chattered from the terror of what I'd just experienced. I clutched the blanket to my chin. The witches had been right. They had seen me, but the scarier part was that I had no control of my body apparently. Was I sleepwalking? A side effect from the shock of dying?

Curling in on myself, I decided that I had to speak to someone about this soon, because it was clear this wasn't a one-off incident. Something was very broken inside me.

* * *

THAT MORNING, I made the decision to pay the three men who had turned my life upside down a visit. A secret, spying kind of visit to get to know them better, when they would show me the side of them I wanted to see. The time I spent with Alaric had given me a lot to think about during my delivery shift. He had revealed a softer side of himself, but I kept wondering if that was him pitying me or if he was genuine.

I hated not knowing the truth, so I was prepared to play the sleuth. I had seen a part of Alaric that surprised me. Though, he still kept secrets, and I wasn't finished diving into what he hid. The same applied to Keon. From what I'd learned, he was a ticking time bomb, but there was more to him I wanted to learn.

After storing the cart away in the kitchen and cleaning up, I headed out into the empty mess hall. Quick steps carried me deeper into the penitentiary. I scaled the steps up to the next floor and kept my head low. I learned that making eye contact was an invitation for war. Plus, I'd also done well so far to avoid the two witches, though I had no doubt they would be blaming me for the feathery mess in their cell.

A shiver gripped me when I remembered what I'd done, but I shoved those thoughts aside. I couldn't think about it without giving myself a panic attack. I'd seek help soon, but right now, I wanted to focus on the task at hand and not freak myself out that I was losing control.

Seth's door came into view up ahead, and my stomach tightened. I was still unable to get the image out of my mind of him kissing the gorgeous fae. The muscles in my shoulders twitched at how perfect she had been. Perfect white hair. Perfect lips. Perfect body. I hated her, and I didn't even know her.

A guard marched toward me, and I bristled as his eyes traced the length of my body. He passed without a word. A few steps later, I glanced behind me to make sure he was gone. Then I raced up to Seth's barred door. I pressed myself flat against the wall near the entrance, taking a deep breath, then stuck my head out to look inside. A dim light filled the space, and near the bed, Seth crouched on the floor, facing away from me. By the movement of his arm, I could only imagine he was drawing.

There was something painful about watching such a powerful fae stuck in a room and drawing on the floor to stop from going insane. I remembered the last image of his I found of me. The delicate lines, the beauty with which he'd captured me. Why would he have done that, with no intention of me finding the illustration, if he had a fiancée the whole time?

I furrowed my brow and drew away, unsure how to solve the mystery that was Seth. The only real answer lay in asking him directly. As cowardly as it sounded, I didn't have it in me to confront him about it or hear him admit he was committed to someone else.

I wanted to imagine it was me he painted on the floor, but for all I knew, it was the ethereal woman he'd held in his arms last.

An ache rose through me, bringing with it the

painful memories I wasn't ready to face. Not yet, so I quietly left him behind and made my way to the farther corridors where many of the packs resided. On my travels with Trevor to deliver meals, he'd revealed passages less traveled that would take me there. If the penitentiary behaved and didn't change hallways, I might be able to avoid the majority of the inmates and come out not far from Alaric's prison cell.

Turning left and right, I moved swiftly in dimly lit stone hallways with no one else around. An eeriness climbed up the back of my legs, which had me speeding. When I emerged from a narrow passage, I stepped out into a familiar hall where Alaric and the snake shifter had first fought.

People were everywhere, the place reminding me of a busy sidewalk on Christmas Eve filled with angry shoppers.

I darted across the hallway and stayed near the wall to not be seen, then made a beeline for Alaric's room. I peered inside as I reached the doorway, only to find it empty.

"He's not home." A deep guttural voice came from behind me, a voice I recognized all too well. A delightful shiver raced up my back as I turned to Laz.

"What are you doing here?" I asked.

He leaned an arm against the wall, staring at me with those deep eyes that brought back so many memories of our time together. An escape from everything else, and yet in his presence, my body flared awake with arousal. Those perfect full lips curled upward into a mischievous grin. Everything about him called to me when it shouldn't have.

"You are in my quarter, darling. And I'm surprised you're back here after what happened last time."

I stiffened, well aware of what he referred to, but instead, I wrenched my head to the side and studied everyone minding their own business for a change. "It looks like the rest of the prison to me. Plus, I don't run away from fear."

His lips arched wider, and just having him stare at me with such admiration had me picturing that mouth, warm and soft, demanding across my mouth. Taking what he wanted. My nipples hardened in response.

I pushed away from him. "Have fun," I said and turned to walk away.

Suddenly, he snatched the back of my neck and hauled me toward him. Before I had the chance to protest, his lips brushed against mine, tender at first, then hard. With his other arm sweeping across my back, he walked me backward and right into Alaric's prison cell.

My back hit the wall, and his body crushed mine. Hands drifted up my arms. Something overcame me, and I lifted my hands, cupping his face and kissing him back. I hadn't come here to make out with Laz, but I worried I'd opened up a Pandora's box when it came to him.

Finally, we broke apart and reality crashed through me that I was kissing the hellhound in Alaric's room. He would go ballistic if he found out, and the guy had connections everywhere. Fuck. I didn't want Laz dead.

I shoved him off me, then slapped his face, anger rising through me. "Why did you do that?"

He didn't even seem to feel my hand striking his cheek, but instead grinned. "Little one, a small pack of snake shifters were headed down this hallway, and you're not exactly their favorite person. So count yourself lucky I just saved that sweet ass of yours."

I glanced outside to people casually walking past the prison cell. My lips ached from his hard kiss, my body straining for him, and my nipples grazing the fabric of my bra each time I moved only added to the growing desire.

"You did that for me?" I asked, turning to look at him as he ran a hand through his hair. And the bulge in his pants didn't go amiss either. He was a beast of a man in size all around.

"You seem surprised."

"Well, not many people in the penitentiary go out of their way to help others." I shrugged, eyeing Alaric's room. The simple bed. Clothes folded perfectly on the shelves in the back. Two books sat on the table near the bed, and not much else. Nothing personal, though I didn't know why it surprised me. If he had the secret television room, why would he leave anything personal in the room?

"Want to see something?" Laz asked.

I narrowed my eyes at him. "Is that some

euphemism for..." I lowered my gaze to the way his cock tented his orange pants.

He laughed, the sound a cross between a howl and the deep kind of noise that came from the pit of his stomach. Then he reached down and groped himself. "My one-eyed monster is yours whenever you want him, babe." He cocked an eyebrow. "But that's not what I meant."

"What then?" On purpose, I ignored his comment about him offering himself to me whenever, refusing to flirt before I ended up in Alaric's bed with him.

His hand slid into mine, and he guided me outside. "Follow me."

Was I being a fool in getting close to him, holding his hand in public? Technically, I wasn't with any of the other guys, but the three of them were extremely possessive, so me grasping onto Laz's hand might lead to war.

When I tried to pull free, his hold tightened, swinging his gaze over his shoulder at me. "Better to be safe than sorry."

Of course he was referring to the snake shifters, and I found myself looking at everyone who looked my way in case someone intended to hurt me. Maybe coming here wasn't such a good idea after all.

I tracked alongside Laz, who held me close, until he took a sharp left with me in tow. He was opening a door, and in seconds, we stepped outdoors.

Fresh wind blew through my hair, and it was the most beautiful sensation. Indoors felt like a sardine can with stuffy air. I took in several deep mouthfuls, bathing in the natural light before looking around at a yard covered in grass nestled between two lofty buildings. The sun remained hidden behind heavy clouds, and I stared at what looked like small garden patches that had long been overgrown with weeds.

"What is this place?"

"Something I want to offer you to use when you need it. It originated as a small project by the prison doc, but it was quickly shut down by the warden. He doesn't believe in rehabilitation." He stuck his hand into his pocket and pulled out a small metal key, then placed it into my palm. "Stole it ages ago, and I come out here to calm down, otherwise I have terrible sleep walking problems. I walk into the wall over and over. You know how many times I woke up in a puddle of my own blood? But now I want you to have it."

His words piqued my interest instantly. "You sleep walk as well?" I curled my fingers around the key, feeling the warmth of the metal from his touch. "Thanks for the key by the way. That's really sweet of you." I slipped it into the pocket of my pants.

"Seems we have more in common than I'd realized."

An excitement rose through me. "How do you stop it?" I asked. "Did you ever find yourself out of your cell and doing strange shit?"

The way he looked at me said none of those things applied to him. "Generally, I just walk and bump into things since I'm closed in my room."

"Oh." I glanced away, hating that I let myself have high hopes so quickly.

"Hey." He touched my shoulder. "Tell me more about your experiences. Maybe we can help each other."

I lifted my head and stared back at him. What did I have to lose by telling him the truth? I had no idea what was going on, and maybe he'd have some insight.

I moved to a soft patch of grass and sat down, Laz doing the same, leaning his arms over his bent knees.

"This stays just between us, all right?"

He nodded.

"I don't really understand it. I've never walked in my sleep before, but last night, I woke up outside my prison cell. And my door was open like someone had unlocked it for me once the lights went out. Worse part, I think I broke into someone else's room and plucked their taxidermic raven."

He frowned. "You said plucked, right?"

I rolled my eyes and whacked him in the arm. "There were black feathers everywhere. And yesterday, those women accused me of stealing other stuff from them. That's strange, right?"

"You sure you were sleepwalking and someone isn't pranking you?"

I blinked up at him as his words sank in. I had contemplated the idea, and it would explain a lot. "Maybe those witches set me up? But why? I don't even know them."

"Maybe leave some kind of trap in your door," he suggested.

"Right, so then the two of us can sleepwalk together? I can see it now."

"Wonder if there's such a thing as sleep sex. If I leave you horny enough, then you'll break into my room instead of someone else's. I like this plan." That time, I laughed at his fantasy, though my lips still tingled from his mouth on mine earlier. The guy knew how to damn kiss.

I lifted my head to the blue sky bruised with dark clouds as though a storm approached. I missed seeing the weather, experiencing rain, the sun burning down on my shoulders. The key in my pocket was a reminder that Laz had given me something special. A small escape when I wanted nothing more than to get away.

It was a strange thing to feel comfortable while in someone's company you barely knew. But Laz had a way of calming me. I leaned back on my arms and crossed my legs at my ankles. "How'd you end up in here?" I asked.

"I was framed by my second in command," he answered, lowering his head, his back curling forward. "The bastard wanted my pack, so he killed my mate and planted her dead body to frame me. Before I knew it, the cops had busted down my door and I was thrown into this place."

"Fuck. I'm so sorry. That is horrific." My stomach rolled. "How could he do that?"

"The worst part is that I never saw it coming. It

happened seven years ago, and I still burn with rage to destroy him."

Soul-crushing, his recount throttled me. I pushed up and rubbed his back. I had no words to say about something so horrific. We sat in silence, and I remained by his side. Goosebumps raced up my arms, the hair standing on end along my arms to imagine experiencing such devastating betrayal.

"Laz," I said after a while. "Are you okay?"

There was no response a first, then he stood. "We should head back inside." His voice cracked, then he cleared his throat.

He leaned down and took my hand, hauling me to my feet. "Don't worry about me, babe. I'm perfect. Once I get out of this joint, I have someone to hunt down and obliterate."

I was lost for words and wished I knew the right thing to say.

Back indoors, I pulled the locked door shut, and Laz led me back to the main part of the prison where my cell lay.

"I'll see you hopefully in my room tonight." He winked so sexily, my legs trembled, then he strolled back the way we came, vanishing into the crowd. He was definitely not what I expected. Seemed no one was.

Someone snatched my hair and yanked backward, forcing me to cry out and retreat with quick steps to avoid falling over.

"Bitch, I know it was you," a croaky female's voice came.

I twisted around, grabbing my hair and managed to wrench myself free. I swallowed the lump in the back of my throat and hated how it was one thing after another here.

Raising myself, I faced the short-haired witch glaring in my direction, and if her stare could kill me, I'd be pinned to the wall already, dead.

"You killed our bird. I know you did," she bellowed.

"You've got me confused with someone else, I told you before." I curled my hands into fists, ready to fight if required.

Instead, a sudden explosion of cheering sounded from behind me. In a sudden flurry of busybodies, so many of the prisoners shoved past us to get to the commotion. Elbows in my ribs. Trodden on feet. I was pushed backward, but with the distance between the witch and I growing, I didn't resist the push and tug. I really didn't know what to tell the woman until I worked out what the hell was wrong with me.

Pivoting around to see where the masses were taking me, I came to where a group of guys were in a vicious brawl. It seemed to be happening daily, and everyone craved them for entertainment. I might have turned around if it wasn't for Keon slicing through the masses and jumping in to stop the battle.

He had no clue I'd joined the audience, but seeing him move, he reminded me of a wolf. Swift and predatory, he knew exactly what he was doing. He went for the largest guy first, locked an arm around his neck, and wrenched him backward, then drove a knee into his back, sending him to his knees. The crowd seemed to be cheering Keon more than the fighters. And by the look of his grin, he was right in his element. He loved fighting, and he knew he was so damn strong, I wasn't sure anyone stood a chance against him. With each punch he delivered, he grinned wider, taking joy from his punishment. I wouldn't have thought guards were allowed to beat up prisoners as he was doing, but no one stopped him. Not even the three other guards watching.

Alaric was right about Keon being a wild cannon. I withdrew through the mob and rushed back to my cell, just wanting to hide from everything and sleep. Right then, I was reminded too much of Keon fighting before he turned into his demon side. How far did he have to push himself before he lost control and killed someone else?

CHAPTER 9

SELENA

My whole body was sore from my most recent wakeup underneath a table in the cafeteria. I'd woken up when someone had clanged a tray full of food right above where I was sleeping.

I shrieked when I opened my eyes and realized once again, I wasn't in my bed. Adrenaline coursed through me as a group of prisoners sat down right around where I'd found myself. I narrowly missed being kicked in the ribs as one of them guffawed loudly as he swung his legs underneath him.

I lay there for a moment, examining the old food crusted under the table, wondering how the heck I was going to explain myself if I suddenly popped out from under the table.

Not only was I freaking out because I'd woken up somewhere other than my cell, I was also freaking out at the fact that I hadn't woken up before this.

The cafeteria was loud already.

Meaning that we were well into breakfast, and I definitely should have woken up before this.

What if it wasn't breakfast? What if it was lunch?

Just then, I realized that not only was I underneath a disgusting cafeteria table, but my clothes were also soaking wet, like I'd gone swimming during the night.

I shifted out of the way of another swinging foot and cringed when I felt something slimy squish against my neck. These floors had obviously not been cleaned last night. Or maybe ever.

Another person sat down, and this time, I didn't miss the kick to my leg.

I gasped in pain, and the confused face of a guy I'd seen before, rumored to be a bear shifter, suddenly appeared underneath the table. His mouth dropped open as he saw me there.

I waved and took the opportunity to scoot out from under the table as smoothly as I could. What felt like a million eyes were suddenly on me. The area around the table was silent for a moment before whispers and laughter erupted.

I stood up, trying to look as confident as I could, despite the fact that I knew there was last night's casserole squished in my hair and I was soaking wet.

I kept my chin held high as I strode quickly over to the door. Laz appeared beside me, and I held up a hand before he could say anything and he wisely kept silent. I'm sure the smell emanating from me was a great deterrent as well.

I was about to turn right to go to my cell when I

heard what sounded like a pack of prisoners coming down the main hall. Not wanting to run into so many people, I turned left and jogged down a hall and then another, turning down what I thought would connect me to another hallway that led to my cell.

It only took me a minute or two to realize I in fact had never been down this hallway. I stopped and leaned against the wall, fighting the urge to bash my head against the wall in frustration. I didn't need a headache or a concussion on top of everything else.

A sign for a women's shower room just down the hall caught my attention. Thinking that I could clean up a bit before finding my way back into my cell, I hurried over, thinking it was odd there weren't any guards around.

There was no one around, and I couldn't hear any of the showers running. I walked over to the sinks and let out a squeak when I saw myself. It was a good thing that I didn't care what anyone in this prison thought about me, because I looked like I had been ridden hard and put away wet.

I was literally soaked. Clumps of food were bunched in my hair like I was going for a sort of epicurean dreadlock look. There was ketchup somehow smeared on my cheek. Although I'd gone to bed in my nightclothes, I'd somehow ended up back in my prison jumpsuit. It was smeared with food stains and of course soaking wet.

Sighing in distress, fear over what was happening to me searing through my veins, I headed to the showers.

Looking around, I noted that these showers were unusually clean. Dusty but clean...like they hadn't been used in a very long time. Usually, the showers were littered with debris and questionable items. There was nothing like that here.

Everything was spotless.

Deciding not to look a gift horse in the mouth, I wandered over to the showers. They were dusty as well, but clean.

Weird.

I slipped off my disgusting, food-laden jumpsuit and turned on the shower, not bothering to wait until the water warmed up, because that was never going to happen.

The warden was all about torturing his subjects, and a cold shower was just another way that he did so.

"Has no one ever taught you how to eat? The food is supposed to go in your mouth, not on your clothes," a miffed English accented voice sounded from beside me unexpectedly.

I screamed and jumped away, slamming into the side of the shower stall farthest from where the voice had come from.

I looked around wildly.

There was no one there.

"Boo," the voice whispered from behind me, which should have been impossible, because behind me was the freaking wall.

I ran through the freezing cold spray of water and out into the open areas in front of the showers. I frantically tried to cover myself as I looked around for the asshole who'd just joined me in the shower. There was a clump of mashed potato between my toes that must have dropped from my hair and I tried to shake it off as I glared around the room.

I couldn't see anyone.

Still naked, I held my hand across my chest to try and support my breasts as I ran frantically to each stall, trying to find out who was in here with me.

"My dear, a lady does not run around naked as the day they were born in public. It's just not polite."

Where was that voice coming from?

"Who are you?" I screeched, shivering from my brief, glacial shower and beyond pissed.

A figure suddenly materialized a foot away from my face, and I fell backwards to the tiled floor in shock.

There was a ghost standing in front of me. The ghost of a tight-ass headmistress who probably sipped tea with her pinkie out by the looks of it. Her skin was a shimmering, barely translucent silver in color, and she had black hair that was pulled back in a severe bun parted down the middle. I had the sudden urge to tell her that not many people could pull off the middle part, but I refrained.

She was wearing spectacles low on her nose, and her lips were pursed as she studied me like I was a cockroach she'd found crawling around on her freshly cleaned floor. The ghost was wearing a black Victorian dress, with a white frilly collar that was almost to her chin, and went down past her ankles. She looked like she'd never smiled in her life, and I expected at any minute for her to pull out a ruler and rap me across the knuckles.

"And now you're staring at me. Have you no manners whatsoever, young lady?"

I continued to stare, flabbergasted. Just when I thought that I'd seen just about everything I could see in the prison, here I was completely naked on the bathroom floor getting lectured by a schoolmarm.

Who was I right now?

"If we're talking about being rude, do you think you could possibly avert your eyes while I finish showering?" I asked her, trying to keep the amusement and annoyance out of my voice.

I would just leave, but something told me this ghost was relatively harmless, and the mashed potatoes in between my toes were driving me crazy.

"Well, I do say," she sniffed. "You were the one who came into my home without permission. I was just protecting myself from intruders, as any woman would do."

"Right," I answered, not sure what to say. "I'm just going to be in there, if you could stay out for just a bit."

She sniffed again but didn't say anything, so I took that to mean she was going to let me shower.

Trying to cover as much of my skin as possible I darted back into the shower and under the still running spray.

"Your hair is absolutely atrocious. You need a hair mask and a trim immediately. How do you expect to catch a man when you look like a bedraggled rat?" came the ghost's voice from outside the door. I guessed that was an improvement from her voice coming from inside the shower.

I ignored her, because arguing with a ghost about my hair routine seemed a little crazy and I'd reached my threshold of crazy for the day.

"Well, I never! She comes into my house, uses my shower, and then ignores me when I try and engage in polite conversation," she muttered to herself.

"I can hear you," I finally told her through the shower door when the murmuring continued. I was pretty sure she'd just called me a cow.

"Heard what?" she asked innocently.

I snorted and scrubbed harder at my hair. There was a jelly-like substance stuck in my strands on the back of my head, and it seemed to be impervious to water.

Something was dropped on my head just then.

"Ouch," I yelped as it clattered to the ground. Peering down to see what the ghost had dropped on my head, I was shocked to see it was shampoo. Fancy shampoo in fact.

"Use that. I won't be able to look at you with your hair like that. It's too distracting," she said through the door.

I stared at the door suspiciously as I leaned to grab the shampoo. "Can you see through that door?"

Another huff.

I was tempted to just get out of the shower then, but

the shampoo was really nice and my hair was still stuck together in the back. I quickly squirted a glob of shampoo in my hand and went to work, wondering about the mechanics of a ghost being able to pick up a plastic bottle while I scrubbed.

"You're wasting water. In my day, my students were allowed five minutes to bathe! Five minutes! You're at least fifteen minutes in. You are not the Queen of England."

Annoyed, I shut off the water, just as I realized that I didn't have a towel.

As if she was reading my mind, a towel flew over the door.

When I didn't say anything, she huffed again. "Thank you is also something a lady must always say."

"Thank you," I muttered absentmindedly as I stared at my filthy, soaked jumpsuit in disgust. I was going to need to shower again after putting that on.

Cringing, I slipped it on and opened the door to leave the stall. The ghost appeared right in front of me, and I stumbled backward once again.

Her lips were pursed even more than before as she scrutinized me closely. It looked like she'd just stuffed a lemon in her mouth and the sour taste was almost too much for her to bear.

"I let you use my shower. I give you shampoo. And this is how you repay me," she said, casting a hand over her forehead like my appearance was about to make her faint. "And you smell. You're the only creature I've encountered that somehow smells worse after a shower than you did before."

"I'm just going to be going now," I told her, slipping around her to head towards the exit, since something told me she wouldn't take kindly to me walking through her.

"It's decided, we'll begin lessons immediately," she told me after I'd only made it a few steps.

I froze. "That won't be necessary," I replied with an uneasy laugh. "I'm perfectly polite most of the time. You caught me at a sort of inopportune time. I'm not usually rude when I'm naked."

I was cracking myself up today.

I resumed walking towards the exit when the ghost appeared in front of me. I grasped at my chest. "Can you stop doing that? You're going to give me a heart attack."

"Well it would be a better way to go than an electric chair," she sniffed indignantly, shaking her pointer finger at me.

Well, that was unexpected. I didn't think I wanted to know what this woman had done to garner the electric chair at a place like Nightmare Penitentiary. I mean, there were hosts of murderers walking these halls and sleeping in these cells. And none of them were headed for the chair.

"I'm just going to be heading out now," I told her, side-stepping around her once again and practically running to the exit.

"Your form's all wrong," she called after me.

I made it back in the hallway and headed over to where I'd made the wrong turn what felt like hours ago.

I'd just taken a breath in relief when, with a *pop*, the ghost appeared right in front of me again.

Her face was somehow more of a pink than a silver, and a strand of her previously perfect hair had fallen into her face. She was exhaling loudly. Which was a little odd because I was pretty sure that ghosts didn't breathe. She was acting like she'd had to run after me.

"Well, I never!" she howled.

"Why are you following me?" I snapped. I'd woken up under a cafeteria table wet and covered in food, taken an ice-cold shower, and now I was still wet and my clothes were still covered in food. I was not in the mood to be stalked by a ghost.

I took off on a dash, not caring about the prisoners who stared at me as I passed by. I slammed my cell door shut behind me and flopped against the wall, taking a deep breath.

"I suppose this will have to do," came the ghost's voice from my cot.

I let out a little scream. She was lounging on my bed, her arms behind her head, as she took in the room with that same revulsion-filled look that she'd had the entire time.

"What are you doing here?" I screeched.

"Well I can't exactly give you lessons from across the prison, can I?" she responded calmly.

"Get out! Get out! Get out!" I yelled, officially done.

She stared at me, her mouth gaping in a very unladylike manner.

"I won't stay where I'm not wanted," she finally said in a very pissed-off voice before she disappeared with another loud *pop*.

I waited for a second, expecting her to appear again at any second. But my cell remained blissfully quiet, besides the usual howls and screams from the miserable prisoners around me.

I stripped off my jumpsuit and grabbed a clean one before laying on my bed. I was exhausted, but I was afraid to close my eyes. Where would I wake up next?

What was happening to me?

Despite my best efforts to keep awake, sleep's call was finally too strong, and I slipped away into dreamland, where a stern faced Mary Poppins figure was ready to deliver a lecture to me.

* * *

I WOKE up the next morning after somehow sleeping for twelve hours straight, relieved to see that I was still on my cot in my cell. I sat up, grateful before I looked down and saw that my shoes were covered in mud.

I didn't go outside in this prison. And the sections of the prison with dirt floors were definitely not places that I would want to find myself during the day, let alone while I was sleepwalking at night. Even the garden area Laz showed me was completely covered in overgrown grass and weeds, not mud.

Before I could freak out appropriately, my cell door clanged open and a guard appeared. "Time to go to the crazy doctor," he grinned savagely, the effect minimized by the fact that he was missing at least two teeth.

I groaned and flopped backwards as he cackled.

"Give me a second," I told him as I got up from the bed, steadfastly keeping my gaze averted from my muddy shoes until I had to put them on.

This guard was not one of the okay ones, and he watched me hungrily the whole time I changed, although I did my best to cover myself up.

I felt nothing but dread as we walked to the prison psychiatrist's office. My mandatory "counseling" sessions, as they were called, had thankfully been few and far between. Evidently, there were people in this prison who needed sessions more than me. Imagine that. There was no rhyme or reason to when a session was scheduled, so there was no way to anticipate them.

I sighed as I saw the familiar *Prison Psychiatrist* sign on the door. Like usual, the guard knocked on the door, and we waited for the doctor to call out for me to come in.

Taking a deep breath, I tried to walk confidently into the room and not give the lady any reasons to schedule more of these. The doctor spent most of the time watching me closely as she prodded me with quiet questions. It felt like she could see all the way beneath my skin.

She didn't say anything as I walked towards the couch. She just stared at me quietly. Her lipstick today was her usual red, and she was dressed in a sleek, black pantsuit that I was immediately jealous of. What would it be like to wear something other than a jumpsuit?

I settled down into the couch, wondering how long our session would be today.

Before saying anything else, she grabbed one of her long cigarettes from the tin box next to her, lit the end with a match and took a long drag, closing her eyes almost in relief as she did so.

"You've had quite the eventful last few months," she said quietly as she opened a file on the table in front of her that I assumed was mine. Strangely, it looked far thicker than it had been last time.

"Most recently, you had a near-death experience," she commented calmly without looking up from the file.

She hadn't said it like she was asking a question, so I just remained quiet. Dr. Maynard was silent as she continued to read whatever was in my file. I tried to surreptitiously read what was on the page. Everything that had happened at this place had definitely been unsanctioned, making me wonder who was watching me and how closely were they doing it.

With a small exhale of breath, she closed the file, as if whatever she'd read disappointed her. She looked up at me, her unnerving empty eyes once again staring at me closely.

"How have you been feeling since waking up?" she asked.

I opened my mouth to answer that I'd been fine, but

right before I did that, I hesitated. Would it really be that bad to mention some of what had been happening since I'd woken up? "Things have been mostly fine," I began slowly. "But there have been some strange things…just a few."

Dr. Maynard leaned forward, the first show of interest she'd ever had when I'd come in here. "Go on," she pressed in her quiet voice.

"My skin doesn't feel like my own," I whispered. "And…I've been waking up in strange places with no idea of how I've gotten there."

The words flooded out then. I told her everything that occurred, including waking up this morning with mud on my shoes.

She was nodding as I finished, not looking surprised or worried at all by everything I'd just told her. "It sounds like you brought back some kind of spirit with you," she told me. It was frustrating how placid she looked as she said that, like I'd mentioned I wanted baked beans for lunch instead of telling her all the strange shit that was happening to me.

"A spirit?" I asked, unease shooting down my spine.

"It's hard for them to get here otherwise, so they're always grateful when someone visits the afterworld briefly before being called back. They just hitch a ride," she explained with a small smile, using her fingers to mimic walking.

Her nonchalant manner was about to drive me over the edge. I was cranky enough as it was…and also exhausted, which was strange with all the sleep I'd gotten last night.

"Your emotions have probably been a little extreme as well. And I would assume by the bags under your eyes that you're also feeling tired."

I nodded stiffly.

"What you're experiencing at night is probably the spirit taking over. When you're sleeping, you're obviously in a weakened state, which leaves your body open for the spirit to take control. Think of your nightly sojourns as the spirit exploring its new space."

I looked at her in shock. "Is there anything I can do?" I practically screeched at her, panic laced through my words.

"Well I'm sure the warden has something that would get rid of it. I'd bet there's some kind of trinket in his office that would banish it."

I choked at the thought of the warden being the answer to my problems. He was the cause of most of them. "So will you talk to the warden for me?" I asked, a plea leaking through my voice.

She laughed, the sound a small tinkle and barely audible. "The warden would never help a prisoner, Selena." The creepy psychiatrist then took another long drag of her cigarette.

"Well then what can I do?"

She stood up and smoothed down her pants.

"I think this has been a good session, and you've made a lot of progress. We'll schedule another meeting soon," she told me, gesturing to the door.

I sat there shocked for a moment, thinking that there was no way that she could really be dismissing me like this. I'd taken a chance, opened up to her... actually needing help.

And she was kicking me out?

Worse honestly, was the fact that she laughed.

I stood up shakily, fighting the urge to cry. The guard was waiting for me, looking bored. Dr. Maynard closed the door quietly behind me, and I swear as I walked down the hall, I could hear her faint tinkle of laughter following me all the way back to my cell.

What a bitch.

CHAPTER 10

SELENA

I stared up at the ceiling, idly watching water drip down beside me. Was the spirit or ghost watching the same thing right now? How did it work? Was it staring out of my eyes, or did it lie dormant until I was asleep and that was when it came alive?

It was hard to resist the urge to claw at my skin, to want to tear it open and drag whatever was there out of me. I trembled lying there. It was hard to describe how it felt, this knowledge that something was wrong with me. That you weren't alone. An eerie feeling slid across my collarbone like someone was watching me.

I flew off the bed and started pacing the cell. I was so freaking tired. It felt like I could sleep forever.

But I couldn't let that happen.

"A trinket in the warden's office," I whispered to myself, probably sounding crazy if anyone was listening. "Of course it would be in his office. It might as well be on the moon."

A little squeak distracted me from my spiraling thoughts. I looked down to see my little mouse friend standing on his hind legs, holding what looked like a chocolate M&M. I took it politely and then set it on my bed.

"I'm saving it for later," I told the mouse, not wanting to look ungrateful. But while I was crazy enough to talk to a mouse, I wasn't crazy enough to eat food that the mouse was holding. Even if it was the only chocolate that I'd seen in the place, besides the bar Alaric offered me the other day or Keon sneaking me some from outside the prison.

The mouse squeaked something that sounded like it was trying to reassure me. I leaned down and stroked the top of his head softly.

"You're all I have left in here, buddy," I whispered to it.

He squeaked something else and nuzzled my finger. Suddenly, he froze and sniffed the air. Whatever he smelled seemed to terrify him, because his entire body shook and he ran away like a pack of cats were after him.

I went back to pacing.

After a while, I started to drag. I could literally feel the energy being rapidly sucked out of me. I stumbled to my cot.

"Can't fall asleep," I murmured, slapping myself in the face.

I put my head right under the dirty water, hoping that the cold water splashing my skin would help me stay awake.

But it was a losing battle. I went from sitting down to falling over on my cot. It was like an iron weight was suddenly covering my entire body, weighing me down.

It wasn't long before I drifted into a dreamless sleep.

MY EYES SHOT open as I woke up to the sensation of falling. I put out my hands in front of me just as I fell into what felt like a puddle of sludge. It was pitch black wherever I was, and the smell was completely overwhelming, like someone had gathered up the perfect concoction of feces, vomit, and rotten food and then mixed it all together.

I retched at the smell, nothing coming up since I hadn't eaten in who knows when.

Tears filled my eyes as I tried to feel around for where I'd found myself. "Not the dark, not the dark," I said hysterically as I began to inch forward. I hated pitch blackness, it came from when I was younger and my mother would wake me up in the middle of the night because of some kind of infraction she'd come up with that I'd done earlier in the day. I took to plugging in a night light because it was much less frightening to see what was attacking you than to have swings coming at you in complete darkness.

That fear of darkness stayed with me as I grew up. And it was certainly not doing me any favors right now.

Feeling around, it seemed like I was in some kind of tube, a tunnel of sorts. With the smell, I was pretty sure that I found myself in a sewer tunnel.

How in the world did the ghost get me in this?

I inched along, not understanding how it was possible that there couldn't even be an inkling of light ahead of me.

I began to rap "Lose Yourself" by Eminem out loud to try and distract myself from the smell and the lack of light. The tunnel wasn't tall enough for me to stand up, so I had to crawl my way through it. The way that I'd woken up had made it seem as though I'd dropped from the ceiling, but when I tried to feel around, I didn't find any type of opening. Since I had no clue where I'd come from, I picked the direction that the sludge seemed to be moving and kept going.

"Knees weak, arms are heavy," I rapped as something brushed against my leg.

It's just a piece of trash, it's just a piece of trash, I chanted because if I allowed myself to think for one second that there was something alive in this tunnel with me, I would lose my mind for real. My arms slipped, and I barely caught myself before I landed face first in the toxic mess surrounding me. As it was, I splashed some of the sludge on my face and once again found myself retching from the hideous smell. If I ever got out of this tunnel, I might end up dying just because of the toxic fumes this stuff was giving off.

One inch at a time I went, something continued to brush against my body as I moved forward. I'd just settled into a rhythm and reached the end of the song... when it happened.

Whatever was in my body chose that moment to make its appearance. Dr. Maynard had said that the ghost made its appearance at night when I was sleeping because that was when my mind was most open for a takeover. But I thought that because I was so tired, so scared, so out of control, my mind became weak enough to let whatever it was in me take control at that moment.

My arms and legs began to move much faster than I'd been able to move before. I screeched, trying to gain control of my limbs as I flew through the tunnel like some kind of deranged spider monkey. I could barely move my fingers, and I certainly didn't have enough control to stop myself. It didn't help that there wasn't anything that I could have grabbed on to, even if it was possible.

"Help me!" I began to scream, knowing that no one would help me but needing to try anyway.

An evil laugh leaped out of my throat just then, and tears came hard and fast. It was confirmed, not that it had really been in dispute prior to this, but whatever was inside of me, it was not something good.

I scrambled around a corner, and the tears became tears of relief because there was a light literally peeking out from the end of the tunnel. I screamed again, thinking that maybe someone could hear me now.

As I scrambled closer to the end of the tunnel, my heart threatening to beat out of my chest, the roar of rushing water drowned out my whimpers and heavy breathing.

The thing inside of me continued to have a stranglehold on my body, and all I could do was let out another scream as it took me right out of the tunnel and down, down, down into what looked like a pond of sewage. I landed in the sludge with a splash, doing everything I could to keep my eyes and mouth closed against the poison that I'd been dunked in.

I began to struggle even more against what had taken hold of me. I finally briefly took back control, and I used the opportunity to break through to the surface, taking a heaving breath of the foul air above the vat of poison.

"Help!" I was able to scream once more, when my body was taken back over and I was dunked once again.

It was trying to drown me, that much was obvious, and the reality sent a shiver racing down my spine.

I continued to battle as hard as I could, breaking the surface intermittently.

But I had no energy left. As I began to sink beneath the surface again, I knew it was over.

Is this when I really died and the spirit got my body?

I was about to have to breathe in the sewage, when

suddenly, a strong pair of arms wrapped themselves around me and I was pulled up to the surface.

I gasped out a desperate breath and clutched onto the arms as much as I could.

"Stay with me, pet," Alaric whispered in my ear, and I let out a whimper of relief. The ghost was completely dormant now that I was in Alaric's arms, and Alaric was able to swim me over to a ladder. He gently moved me farther up his shoulder and then began to climb up the ladder as I held onto him tightly.

There was a landing above the ladder, and we both collapsed onto it, inhaling deep breaths of exhaustion. Alaric kept me wrapped in his arms like I could be yanked away at any minute. Which actually wasn't as far-fetched of a fear as I would have once thought. I was exhausted, but I pulled on his sopping wet shirt, wanting to be as close as possible as well. He was my lifeline. It felt like if he let go of me for even a minute, the ghost would come back and I would be gone this time.

I may have had the suckiest life imaginable up to then, but right now, I felt an extreme urge to live.

"You saved me," I whispered as I looked up at him, very aware of how bad we both smelled but not caring in the least bit.

"This was the reaction I was looking for the last time I saved your life," Alaric said wryly, but there was no anger in his voice, only relief.

I tore my gaze away from his to look at our surroundings for the first time. We were in what looked like a giant cave. There was a waterfall across where I'd come out, except instead of beautiful water it was delivering a steady stream of dark brown water. The tunnel I must have fallen out of was situated into the rock wall, at least twenty feet above the pool of muck I'd fallen into.

I trembled just looking at it all. "How did you find me?" I asked in wonder, turning my attention back to him.

He took a deep breath and wrinkled his forehead as he answered. "I don't know," he said slowly, shaking his head slightly in confusion. "I was sleeping, and I woke up to your scream echoing in my head. It sounded so real, and it kept happening. I knew that it had to be real. I broke out of my cell, and it was like there was a rope connecting me to you, I knew where you were."

He shook then, his gaze growing distant as if he was thinking hard about something.

"I broke through that door and saw you thrashing in the water. And then you disappeared. And I just knew...if I didn't get to you right then, I'd never see you again." His body trembled again, and he closed his eyes like he was in pain. His face crumpled up, and he pursed his lips, trying to get control of his emotions.

His eyes flew open then, and I gasped at the love that I saw in his eyes. There was no sign of the cocky, ego-maniac, sex-god in his gaze. There was only complete devotion.

He pulled me into his still quivering arms, and we took comfort in each other's embrace.

It took a while for us to calm down, but I knew I'd relaxed when our smell began to get to me.

It was putrid.

I pulled myself away, missing his embrace the second I did so, and wrinkled up my nose as we looked at each other.

"We smell," I said, stating the obvious.

"Like ass," Alaric agreed, and I couldn't help but giggle because he was coated in brown slime...that may or may not be mostly made up of the prisoner's crap. I was sure I looked exactly the same, if not worse.

And then we were both laughing, so hard that tears streamed from my eyes.

It only took a moment for my laughter to turn into sobs. I was so completely done with everything. Alaric's sexy chuckle faded away, and he quickly stood up, scooping me into his arms.

I laid my cheek carefully against his chest and just let myself cry as he got us out of the sewage room. I guessed if I had to cry, it might as well have been up against a hot guy's body. That seemed to be the only upside from my propensity to crying constantly lately.

I didn't watch where we were going and was surprised when he opened a door and we stepped into an opulent bathroom, complete with a giant marble shower and a pedestal tub that could comfortably fit at least four people.

"What is this place?" I gasped, afraid to move as he set me down on the marble floor. Everything was so white and so clean. The last thing I wanted to do was leave poop streaks everywhere by walking to the shower.

"A trade with the warden for procuring a trinket for him," Alaric commented, walking to the shower and turning it on. "He has a few fancy bathrooms throughout the prison that he loans out to people as little boons."

After finding out this bathroom came from the warden, I had no problem sullying it. In fact, it may have been petty, but I tried to splash as much sludge on the floor as I could as I walked to the shower.

Alaric tried to hold onto a grin, I'm sure knowing exactly what I was doing.

There were multiple nozzles in the shower...and the water was hot! Not lukewarm, not icy cold...hot!

I ignored the fact that this shower belonged to the warden and enjoyed the water as it washed away the slime that covered me. The door to the shower opened, and Alaric stepped in.

My gaze danced across his body briefly, because really...what female could resist, before scooting to the side to give him some room.

I found that my anger had quelled quite a bit after his latest act of heroism.

He squirted a big glob of shampoo in his hand that frankly smelled like heaven and then began to massage it into my hair, making me gasp in pleasure.

"You going to tell me how you found yourself in the prison's sewage station, pet?" he murmured as his caresses began to spread from my hair to my shoulders.

I was silent for a moment, wondering if I should tell him. "Something came back with me when I died," I told him quietly.

He froze, his hands gripping me forcefully with a shudder before quietly letting go. "What did you just say?" he growled in a deadly, furious voice.

I shivered, strangely turned on by the anger in his voice.

"And when did you first realize this?"

"Almost from the moment I came back," I whispered reluctantly. "The spirit has been taking over my body when I sleep. I've started waking up in a strange place in the prison every day, with no idea how I got there." I curled my arms around my chest tightly, feeling vulnerable all of a sudden.

"And you didn't feel like you could trust me," he stated, his head dropping as disappointment knifed through his words. He picked his head up and stared at me. "Did you tell the others?" he asked, the word "others" said with thick distaste.

I shook my head. "I told the psychiatrist," I said with a shrug, trying to inject some levity into the situation. "That obviously didn't do much, since I woke up in a tunnel of sewage."

Alaric looked like he was going to kill somebody... possibly Dr. Maynard.

I washed out the shampoo from my hair, since it seemed like he'd forgotten what he'd been doing. His earlier comment about procuring a trinket for the warden hit me in the head like a sledgehammer.

"She said that the warden probably has something that could get the spirit out," I blurted out as I watched his face closely.

"That would make sense," he said, washing his chest off, deep in thought. My gaze drifted across his perfect abs, suddenly thirsting to be able to touch them with my own hands.

The fact that his body could distract me from ghost possession was really saying something.

He took a predatory step towards me suddenly, and I found myself against the shower wall. "You're not going to hide anything from me again," he ordered with a growl.

I could feel him hard against me. Evidently, he wasn't as distracted as I'd thought.

"This is how it's going to work from now on." He suddenly hoisted me up against the wall. My legs wrapped around him as he positioned me. An involuntary moan escaped my lips as he pressed his length against my clit.

"What's going to work?" I gasped out as he started to thrust against me slowly, the soap and water making it an easy, smooth glide.

"You're going to tell me everything. And then I'm going to fix fucking everything," he ordered as his thrusts picked up speed. "I'll get whatever fucking thing we need from that asshole. I'll always take care of you."

His lips were on me then. His mouth claimed mine in a hungry kiss, licking deep into my mouth eagerly and aggressively. He pulled my hips closer to him, bringing me against his hard length. The friction was delicious. Deep, languid, rolling thrusts pushed me closer to the edge I was desperate to fall off of.

Small whimpers spilled from my throat. I needed him. I was desperate for him to drive into me, spreading me open, giving me everything.

My body clenched and throbbed wildly when I finally fell. I buried my face against his neck as I rode it out. Taking a deep breath and wanting more, I pulled my face away and admired what was before me.

He got the message, because he grinned, laying a soft kiss on my lips. Our gazes locked as he pushed in slowly, carefully, like I was the most precious thing to him, gently stretching me. He had an awestruck look, as if this was our first time. Holding still, letting me adjust to his size, his mouth descended on mine, his demanding tongue plunging in. A submissive type of neediness consumed me as I sucked his tongue greedily, whimpering. Long moments later, my hips tilted, my body asking him to move. He drew back, watching my face as he pulled out slowly.

"Missed this so fucking much," he groaned. Then he slammed into me hard, sinking all the way in once again.

The sensation of him stretching me open, completely filling me, was overwhelming. He ground into me hard, trying to get deeper. I felt something bubbling inside me, warming me, consuming me. It was emotional. Intense. I felt possessed. By him. But it felt…right.

He kissed me softly. Tenderly. His lips slowly dragging over mine. "Fuck, you're the most beautiful thing I've ever seen," he whispered, fingertips trailing along my jaw. His gaze met mine again as he started moving, angling his hips, hitting that perfect place inside of me. My head pushed against the shower wall as pleasure raced through every vein in my body.

His hips continued to move, his groans and my screams filling the room. He didn't slow his brutal pace, and he buried his head in the crook of my neck, sucking on the sensitive skin there.

I was overloaded with sensation, and he wasn't finished yet.

He didn't finish for a long, long time.

And the water stayed hot the entire time.

CHAPTER 11

SELENA

*T*here was something to be said about how much my social life had boomed since arriving in Nightmare Penitentiary, and how sad my life had been beforehand.

I walked away from the mess hall from my morning shift, the whole time thinking about how close I'd come to dying again. How lucky I had been that Alaric found and saved me. My mind filled with images of us in the show room, and a tingle raced down my spine. But there was no time to become complacent when I had a ghost trying to kill me.

I had every intention of spying on the guys and uncovering their secrets, except with everything of late, I no longer wanted to be alone. Tensing, I kept walking, figuring I'd have to track down Alaric and see if he's had any luck in tracking down the trinket to eliminate the ghost.

The main hallway was a wide space, and yet there

were people everywhere, chatting and pushing past, meaning I wove around them. Even the great centaur made himself comfortable, sitting down with others in the area, blocking a huge section of the hallway. I noted everyone gave him a wide berth, and I did the same.

I took the steps up to the next floor when I spotted Keon standing with his back to me, leaning a bent arm against the metal railing. His dark guard's uniform fit his strong physique perfectly, following the muscles in his back, the firmness of his ass, the hardness of his thighs. Keon was talking to my little friend, the brown mouse. I couldn't hear the words, but his mouth moved and the critter looked up at him as if understanding.

How strange. Curiosity pushed me forward, and I approached them. Keon placed the mouse on the floor, and the little thing scrambled away.

He straightened, glancing over and meeting my gaze. The corners of his mouth curled upward, his spectacular green eyes glinting at seeing me. What I found strange was he didn't have a hint of a bruise or cut on his face, and I'd just seen him the day before in a brutal fight.

"How are you?" he asked, his voice confident and his posture just as broad and powerful. Yellow light filtering in from fluorescent lights stole the shadows from across his face. Something about his clean face with a whisper of growth across his jawline reminded me of the first time I picked him up at the bar. I'd fallen for his charm from the beginning, and the allure between us only strengthened, despite everything we'd been through.

"Been better," I admitted, then changed the topic, not ready to talk about me. "Is the mouse your pet? He visits me often."

"He's a funny little thing, and you know, he does the rounds, visiting as many of the prisoners as he can. If you ask him for something, sometimes he understands and will bring it to you."

"Really?" Thoughts speared through my mind of all the items he'd brought me, and I wasn't sure if they were in response to what he might have heard me say or just gifts. "How do you know it's not just coincidence?"

"My parents gifted him to me to try and calm my dark urges as a pet or something. I laughed so hard that they thought a mouse could tame me. But turned out he was no ordinary critter. He apparently has some magic in his heritage. He understands so much more than people realize."

"Wow. And you brought him to a prison?"

"Felt sorry for the guy at home alone, restless, running through the whole house without something to do. Here, he has the run of the place. Plus, everyone knows not to hurt him or I'll rip out their throats. It's a fair arrangement."

And he wasn't even kidding on that part.

"Do your parents know about...about the thing inside you?" I whispered, feeling unsure what to call it.

"He's part of my soul, maybe my familiar," he

answered. "My father was a human, and my mother a demon, so I guess I'm the result of such a match."

He ran a hand through his dark hair, though the longer strands just swept back over his brow from his movement. Everything about him hypnotized me, which was so unfair, considering everything he was capable of, yet my body betrayed me over and over when it came to Keon.

He reached out and took my wrist, drawing me closer to him. "Now what brings you to me? You've been avoiding me for so long, it drove me to insanity." He leaned in close, his breath brushing my cheek, warming my ear. "You missed me, didn't you?"

Heat flared across my chest at the dirty intentions dancing in his flirty tone.

But there was still so much unsaid and broken between us that I couldn't let myself fall for his charm that easily. He had killed me, so how was I supposed to process that?

Sure, accidents happen, but this was something else. I'd seen him fight, heard Alaric confirm the same. Keon had control issues with his demonic side.

"Keon," I whispered. "You lost control and killed me. Have you killed this way before?"

He looked at me, a frown morphing over his brow but his fingers around my wrist don't loosen. "Do I scare you?"

"That demon side of you terrifies me." I refused to stop hiding, and maybe the solution had been to speak to him directly, as I knew he had no intention of leaving me alone. The inked stars on my ankle from each time we'd gotten close were proof that our connection wasn't going anywhere.

"We should talk about this somewhere else," he suggested.

I nodded and my heart raced with anticipation of needing to be upfront with him. "I know where we can go." I patted my pocket with Laz's key. I had collected it from my other clothes and taken the key with me, a part of me wanting to go back outside and experience natural light and the cool breeze on my face after my shift.

He kept his eyes on me the entire time. There was something unnerving about how carefully he studied me, as though I might change my mind and run from him. There had never been anyone in my life who personified a stalker more than Keon, and part of me was all right with that. But the monster inside him, I wasn't sure I was comfortable with.

Everything about him screamed an animalistic, testosterone-filled man, who let raw instinct rule him. I'd seen it in his actions, in his eyes.

"Lead the way," he said, and I took the lead toward the stairs, where we merged into the throng of inmates. Normally, I was invisible to them. They bumped into me, shoved me, but with Keon, they parted, respecting him.

By the time we reached the far end of this building, I wondered what would happen if we crossed paths with Alaric or Laz. I didn't want a fight either. I kept scanning the hallways as we traveled until we reached the small passage Laz had shown me. Before long, we were standing outside and once again the sky was bruised gray with clouds and no sign of the sun. Quickly, I shut the door behind us and locked it.

"How do you know about this spot, and who gave you the key?" Keon asked, staring at me when I turned to face him. The wind blew his dark hair off his face, tugging at his uniform, and I breathed harder just staring at how strong he looked, how incredibly handsome he was. But I prayed on the inside that I wasn't making a mistake by having us alone out here to talk.

"A girl doesn't reveal all her secrets." I tucked the key away and wandered down the narrow space flooded with light. "Do you know how much I missed natural light?" The two buildings on either side of us were just stone walls. No windows or doors, throwing us in complete privacy. Up ahead and behind us were lofty metal fences, not revealing what lay beyond them. I didn't care as long as I got fresh air.

"Fair enough," he said and strolled through the overgrown lawn.

I took a seat in a thick patch of grass, crossing my legs, while Keon strolled to the end of the yard, studying the walls for what I guessed was any way others could see us.

When he returned, he dropped to his ass, his legs stretched out before him. He sat across from me. "You asked me earlier if I've killed someone else." He licked his lips. "I want to be honest with you, not scare you.

Growing up, I lost control of my demon three times before you."

I swallowed the boulder in my throat.

There was a moment of silence. Keon stared at me, but before I could find the words lost to me from the utter shock of hearing he'd killed four people, including me, he spoke again.

"It was a very long time ago when the first three took place. I was born different and never fit in. I'm not giving you excuses, just a bit of background. My entire life, I've struggled to feel emotions like most people. You see, the demon side changed me." His lips thinned as he huffed. "Shortly after my birth, my parents split, and my father brought me up. My mother skipped off, maybe to other realms for all I know. And well, humans are not quite cut out to bring up demons."

"I didn't know your mother abandoned you. That's horrible."

He shrugged like he'd dealt with that pain long ago. "You know what I missed about her? It's not the motherly love, but that she never fucking taught me how to control my demon side. Growing up, my demon would slip out of me randomly. My first kill was when I was fourteen. I was home alone, and someone had been breaking into our house."

Silence filled the moment, and I could easily fill in the gaps of what had taken place.

My stomach clenched at the thought of what it must have felt like growing up that way. To have his mother leave him, to have no one teach him how to control his demon side. It broke me to listen to him.

"After the third death, my father put me into an institution, as he didn't know how else to help me. I didn't hate him for his decision. I spent three years there, and I learned so much more from the other patients. Two others had demon parents as well, and they taught me what my mother never did." He glanced at the wall beside us, lost in thought.

"Is your father still alive?" I asked.

"He's in a nursing home, but he's starting to forget things, including me." The sorrow crackling through his voice sliced through me like glass.

When he looked at me, he tilted his head. "Don't feel pity for me. I know exactly what I am, Selena, and I accepted it long ago. A monster."

"No, you're not a monster," I said almost instantly.

"Yes I am," he insisted. "Until the incident with you, I had held my demon under control the only way I could. By feeding it death and souls."

"You let it out on purpose?"

He sighed heavily. "There are two ways. Either it controls me, or I control it. And why do you think I work here? The worst of society resides within these walls. People who don't deserve to live after everything they'd done. They sate my demon so I can keep it under control. I hold control of him when I release him to feed. That's the difference to him taking me over."

I licked my lips, listening to his words. They all made sense and I got it, but he was telling me he killed people regularly. Well, not him, but that thing inside him.

"Around you, I feel things I never have," he said. "Emotions that are so powerful, I can barely stand to be in my own skin some days. And that day I hurt you..." Shadows gathered under his eyes as he breathed in a long inhale. "It's like someone carved my heart right out of my chest. I will live with that agony my whole life that I almost killed the one thing who awakened me. I was so furious that someone else might hurt you and as a result my demon overcame me. I haven't felt that way in a long time."

I shuffled over to sit next to him, our legs touching, and I wrapped an arm around his back, my head pressed to his chest. "I had no idea."

"I don't want secrets between us, and I want you to know the real me."

Nodding my head, I answered, "I know. It will take time for me to get my head around this, but I don't hate you."

"What I feel for you brings out a different side to my demon. It's claimed you as his, and he's a possessive fucking bastard. All he wants is to destroy anyone who touches you."

I pulled back and looked up at him. "That's going to be a problem then. You know how I feel about Alaric and Seth, right? You can't let him hurt them."

"Never in a million years. And I'm making him understand he may need to share you to keep you."

It was strange to hear him talking about sharing me,

but in truth, I'd already been giving a part of myself to these men. I didn't even want to bring up the topic of Laz. Not yet anyway, not until I understood what was going on there. God, I was dating a killer, and the scary part was that I was sort of okay with it. In a strange way, I liked that he removed scum from this world. I mean, didn't we all want to have a little bit of Dexter in us?

Keon placed an arm around me, drawing me closer, and he held me, his breathing slowing.

"I learned that in demon lore, when they fall in love with someone, it's for eternity and call them their fated mate. That's why you have the stars on your ankle from me."

My heart beat faster. Had he just admitted to loving me? Warmth flooded me, and my throat thickened.

I reached over and cupped his face, turning him to look at me. "I grew up in a home void of feelings and emotions, with a vampire who drained the life out of us. But while I had a roof over my head, I never had a mother who told me she loved me." My voice crackled, and something squeezed my heart.

Our brows touched, and a calming sensation came over me. "I'll be your everything, Selena, and I'll never forget to tell you how much you mean to me every day."

"I forgive you," I said and kissed him. But inside, I didn't know if I actually meant it.

Our mouths crashed together, and we kissed chaotically, hungrily. We both came from broken pasts, both searching for something we ended up finding in each other. Something that took me a long while to realize.

His hands roamed over every inch of my body as he desperately pressed me against him. The thickness of his growing cock nestled against my stomach, and I reached down, needing all of him desperately.

He hissed as I stroked his erection over the fabric of his pants. Then suddenly, he broke away and stood, offering me his hand. "Come, let's go to my room," he said.

But I was shaking my head while unbuckling his belt. "No, I want you here, now."

Keon

I watched my kitten crawl over to me and kneel before me like a goddess coming before her god. Her eyes were locked on mine while she placed a hand against my thigh, and her touch against me was an inferno.

My cock was stiff, painful, and needed release. I reached down and unbuttoned my pants, then unzipped myself. My cock sprang out, the cool breeze a welcoming reprieve from the heat swallowing me.

She wrapped her hand around my cock, her fingers barely able to close in around my girth, then she leaned in closer and her delicious rosy mouth slipped over the tip of my erection. Then she licked the tip, flicking it. I groaned, and a rush of thunderous arousal slammed into me.

"That's it. Lick all my pre-cum."

Still gripping me, she traced her lips with the tip of her tongue, and my muscles clenched. Parting her mouth, she took my cock into her mouth.

I hissed, the fire of her wet mouth consuming me. I pushed deeper into her, her tongue flicking over my length. I half expected her to pause, but my little bird took me completely, deep-throating me. She never pulled back, even when I noticed her eyes watering.

I breathed out heavily, seeing her filled with me, working those lips back and forth, her hand on my balls, and it drove me mad.

"Fuck!" I snarled. My heart was in my throat.

She was mine, and I made no fucking apology about taking what belonged to me. Placing a hand to the back of her neck, I fisted her hair, and she didn't push me away. Her gaze was on mine, encouraging me to fuck that sweet little mouth.

I drew in a breath and rocked my hips gently, my pulse racing frantically in my veins. She sucked on me, never pausing, the tip of my cock hitting the back of her throat.

My minx moaned as she meticulously rolled her tongue under my shaft.

Hell, I needed to fuck her. But I loved watching her suck me off.

I drowned in unbearable lust, in arousal that built faster and faster. I was so close to exploding.

Holding onto a chunk of hair at the back of her head, I slid out of her mouth, making a popping sound. She licked her lips and stared up at me with undeniable arousal.

Possessiveness claimed me, and I fell to my knees in front of her, taking her mouth in mine, tasting my own saltiness. I kissed her like I owned every inch of her, taking what I needed. I shoved my hand under her top, and pulled back the top of her bra.

She moaned as I grabbed her breast, squeezing. That perfect little nipple was rock hard in my palm. Her breathing quickened, and her tongue sweeping into my mouth called to me. She wanted me.

I left a trail of kisses down her neck, over her collarbone and skimmed down to her luscious nipple. I drew it into my mouth, tugging at it, gently gnawing.

Her soft cries of pleasure had my breaths speeding up.

I tugged down her pants to her knees, and slipped a hand between her thighs. She was soaking wet, ready for me.

Her hands thread through my hair, fisting it, pulling at it as I pushed a finger into her. I felt the way her body shivered under my touch.

I loved the power I had over her like this. It drove me crazy, and I needed more, more, more. It was never enough.

Releasing her gorgeous, rose tipped breast, I

lavished the same treatment on the other one, then glanced up Selena. She was gnawing on her lower lip, her eyes fluttering upward with her growing desire.

"I need to taste you. To have you come all over my face," I insisted.

"Keon," she breathed, like that was all she was capable of as I bumped two fingers into her tightness.

I pulled my fingers out of her, her slick scent flooding me. I shuddered with desperation to fuck her already. I ripped off my top and lay it on the ground behind her. She took the hint and lay down for me. I grabbed her feet and took off one shoe then the other before tugging her pants and underwear off in one go.

"Show me your tits," I growled as I stood to remove the rest of my clothes. I loved having sex outside where we might be caught, where others might watch, and while this area offered no windows of such possibility, it was close enough to satisfy my fetish.

My beautiful girl lay before me, completely nude, the long grass around her swaying in the breeze. Her nipples stood erect, and as she grinned, she pried her knees open for me.

Her lips glistened, as did the inside of her thighs. My girl was so ready for me. I reached down and parted her inner lips, loving to see her so widely spread, to see her inside exposed to me.

I lowered myself before my goddess and claimed her pussy. I devoured her, licked and sucked until I couldn't breathe, until she was crying out unintelligible things. Pushing my tongue into her, she arched, moaning, her arms stretched out on either side of her, taking fistfuls of grass.

Curling my fingers into the fleshy part of her inner thighs, I swept my tongue over the length of her heat, immersing myself into everything that was Selena.

Pulling at her inner lips, I never stopped, teasing her, driving her to the edge. It didn't take long for her to suddenly release a muffled scream behind her hand so no one heard her. How cute.

Her body convulsed.

I never released her, but took her clit into my mouth and drove a third finger into her pussy, her climax wrecking her. Her thighs clenched on either side of my head, and there was nowhere I'd rather be than locked to her beautiful pussy. She gripped my hair, pushing herself against me, riding me. Hell, she was everything.

Keeping my face buried between her legs, I feasted on her, and the beautiful scent fogged my brain of any other thoughts but staking my claim on her. My breath hitched as my cock twitched, desperate to plunge into her.

Selena meant the world to me. There was no way I could ever let her go, not after opening up to her. I gave her all of me.

When she finally calmed down, collapsed on the ground, I let go of her and pulled up. She lay there, completely spent, spread open and so wet.

"Was that good?" I ran the back of my hand across my mouth.

"I-I c-can't even find words. You are an animal, and I loved every second of it."

"That's what I want to hear. Each time I fuck you, I want you to feel like it's the last thing you'll ever feel."

Her breath hitched. "The things you say turn me on so much."

I laughed and moved closer between her spread legs, palming my cock, before I claimed her.

But she shuffled backward away from me across the lawn, and I frowned. But before I could grab her ankles and drag her back beneath me, she turned over onto her hands and knees. Then she raised that gorgeous ass up high into her air, legs parted.

My sights locked on the way her slit glistened with juices, and my dick hardened to the point of pain with need.

"Please, Keon. I want it doggie style."

I answered, "I'm going to fuck you so hard, you won't walk straight tomorrow."

Selena

HE PALMED MY ASS, the slap coming fast and unexpected right over both cheeks.

I flinched, not expecting him to slap me, but with it came a tantalizing thrill that tracked down my spine.

"You're the devil," I said over my shoulder at Keon

as he grabbed my hips, fingers digging into my flesh as he positioned himself behind me. Something about having my ass in the air and being fully exposed to this man had me shivering with arousal. And I was pretty sure another orgasm was already closing in behind the first.

"Is that any way for a lady to speak?" a British female voice said from in front of me.

My stomach dropped, and I swung my gaze back around to where the ghost sat crossed-legged in front of me. The long grass swayed in the wind, seeming to pass right through her.

"The fuck!"

"Oh, baby girl, I'll fuck you hard," Keon moaned, then drove his cock into me without ceremony. Just slammed in, stretching me so unexpectedly, I screamed.

"Yes, men love screamers," she said, all the while nodding. "You're doing something right at least."

I drowned beneath the sheer size of Keon, which utterly consumed me, the friction as he shoved his cock into me igniting our fire once again.

I rocked back and forth as he slapped into me, and I moaned, yet letting myself fall completely under his spell was difficult while being watched by a psychotic, nosy ghost.

She was on her feet. "Lift your ass higher," she instructed, while standing beside me, hands on her hips, "and tell him to finger you ass."

"Get lost," I growled under my breath.

"Say something?" Keon breathed, his pounding never once ceasing. His energy was unmatched, and when he fucked me, he did so as though he'd been saving himself for me for years.

I adored how he held on so hard to my hips, how he drove deep into me, his moans a delicious song.

"Don't make so many sounds," the ghost continued, and I cried out louder on purpose.

"Oh, he will know you're faking it. I mean, it's clear to me you faked the last orgasm."

I glared at her, mouthing, *fuck off.*

But she didn't seem fazed and pursed her lips, watching Keon slap into me, over and over. My whole body buzzed, and the rise of my climax pushed closer.

"It was deplorable how you sucked his dick by the way," she continued.

I kept my head low as Keon rode me so fast, I could barely catch my breath. In and out, nothing stopped him. I shut my eyes, the excitement building to a point where it was too much. I grasped the grass, holding on as he slammed into me.

"You just took him into your mouth. No licking of his shaft and balls first. Did you never learn the fine art of teasing a man? I need to dig out a book I own. The longer you tease a man, the more he will keep you. I mean, look at this beast humping you, sweating, grunting." She huffed. "You wouldn't catch me rutting him because he just sees you as an easy lay. And while we're on the topic, only prostitutes have sex doggie style, since it offers a lack of intimacy. Do you not like this man? Then why do you let him pluck your flower?"

"Enough," I bellowed, just as an orgasm cut through me, tearing me to the most beautiful shreds of pleasure. My inner walls clenched around him as I contorted with fulfillment.

He never stopped pounding into me, growling his own pleasure. "That's it," he growled. "Squeeze my cock."

I fell apart beneath Keon's touch, and he put me back together. I couldn't stop the groaning sounds that left me, while Keon unleashed deep, gruff noises, pulsing inside me with his own sudden orgasm.

He grasped onto my ass cheeks, squeezing as he pumped his seed into me. He drew them apart, and a cool wind brushed over my exposed parts. Sweat coated me, a drop running down my spine.

Even with my orgasm still pulsing through me, the painful need to have Keon never stopped haunting me.

I opened my eyes and didn't even care that I could no longer see the ghost. I let myself get drunk on Keon. My whole body shook as I floated down from euphoria. I felt his hand on the small of my back, caressing me as he withdrew out of me. Instantly, I missed him and wanted him to fill me again. He might be a stalker, a killer, a dangerous bastard, but he was mine.

He wasted no time in scooping me up like I weighed nothing, and he brought us both to the ground.

I lay cradled in his arms, his chest pressed to my

back, and I kept wondering about how far we had come since we first met, how much we'd gone through. How it was only now that I realized I could never have left Keon. He meant so much more to me than I ever wanted to admit.

"Selena, you fucking destroy me. You are always on my mind, in my dreams, and I can't stop myself from coming to find you every day. It wrecked me to keep my distance."

We stayed like that for so long, and I didn't want to leave. Emotions swirled in my chest, overwhelming me with a strange sensation that made me melt against him. And that was when I realized that I loved Keon back just as much.

We stayed that way for a long pause, and I never wanted to leave. But I also wanted to be completely transparent with Keon. Plus, I needed some help.

"I think I brought back a ghost from the afterlife," I said suddenly. I decided what better time to reveal a bit more about myself than now?

"What do you mean?" he asked, his breath washing over my cheek.

So, I told him everything from me waking up outside my cell, the things I'd stolen, almost getting killed, and what the shrink said about a possible trinket in the warden's office. "I think it's trying to kill me. It seems to appear when I'm sleeping or exhausted."

His arms tightened around me. "Fuck. Then there's only one course of action. Alaric or I will be with you at all times until we retrieve the trinket from the warden. We can't leave you alone."

"You make it sound easy." A thread of hope speared through me that he had some connection that would assist with getting the object to help me.

"Nothing is ever easy in this shit hole, but we have no other option. And I sure as fuck am not going to lose you to a ghost."

I curled my back against him and held onto his arm looped around me, never wanting to let him go. A sense of comfort flared over me, because for the first time in too long, I was starting to feel like it wasn't me against the world.

CHAPTER 12

ALARIC

The rumors were spreading. Precious possessions that prisoners would die to keep safe were going missing.

And all roads lead back to my little possessed siren.

I'd staged two break-ins so far of the warden's office, but nothing had come from it. And we were running out of time.

Keon and I had taken to watching over her at night, but on some nights, somehow, she would disappear in the blink of an eye. Right in front of us, she'd go from sleeping in her bed fitfully to somewhere else in the prison. We both managed to track her down most nights, but the bags under her eyes were growing deeper.

Selena's spirit was a klepto, or maybe it was just trying to get her in trouble. Any time she disappeared, she usually would wake up the next day with something new in her room, something stolen from other prisoners.

Discontent was growing around the penitentiary, and it wasn't the easiest thing to return the stolen goods to their owners and not get caught. Selena had taken to hiding things in various places around her room that we weren't able to get returned, but it was only a matter of time until there would be repercussions and she'd be caught. It was almost like the ghost was seeing how much she could get away with.

I was used to handling a lot at a time, but I usually approached every problem already knowing how I could solve it. The fact that I didn't know what talisman in the warden's office could help, and the fact that I couldn't persuade him to tell me, was a situation I was unaccustomed to.

And it was driving me crazy. I stalked the halls, keeping an ear out for Selena's name to be mentioned, and it was mentioned a lot. I turned a corner and stutter stepped when I saw Selena's little pet, the hellhound, lurking against a wall. He was watching a fight that had broken out between a group of cat shifters. To most people, he would appear disinterested, but I knew better. He was aware of everything around him. And he wasn't hanging in the hallway for his health.

He was waiting for me.

The hellhound didn't look at me when I sidled up to him and leaned against the wall, pretending to watch the fight as well.

"How long are we going to play pretend?" I asked

sarcastically as a prisoner shifted suddenly, swiping a paw full of sharp ebony claws across another prisoner's face.

That probably hurt.

"I want to know what's going on with Selena," he growled. I bristled at her name leaving his lips. It sounded like a caress.

"Why would I tell you anything about her?" I answered calmly.

His body stiffened next to mine, and I smelled something coming off of him that smelled suspiciously like brimstone. The hellhound was obviously very interested in Selena, enough to shatter the calm he was trying to portray.

"She's ignoring me," he admitted reluctantly.

I started to get suspicious. "I wasn't aware you two were close."

"Things have changed recently."

My suspicions grew.

"Is she all right? She seems exhausted every time I see her. Is she sleeping? Eating?" The words rushed out of him like they'd been pent up inside of him. He was desperate to find the answers to his questions. He was a junkie going without his fix.

He'd fucking slept with her.

The hellhound had fucking moved in while the rest of us were on the outs.

A black haze descended on my vision. My hands curled into fists. I was jealous...I was enraged. It felt like hot flames licking at my throat. I'd come to an uneasy acceptance that I was going to have to share with the other two for the time being.

But the hellhound? The loner shifter?

How the hell had that happened right under my nose?

"The way I see it, Selena needs all the help she can get right now," he told me, sensing my fury.

I thought about just how much help Selena needed as another shifter's canines extended and he bit into the jugular of the guy he was fighting. I didn't think the guy was going to come back from that one.

As I watched the shifter begin to chew on the dying man's neck, my anger dampened. I thought about Selena crying in my arms, the fact that Keon and I hadn't been able to protect her, those circles under her eyes.

She did need all the help she could get.

But I hadn't gotten this far in life by trusting everyone around me mindlessly. Maybe there was a way to make his devotion to Selena useful.

I'd send him in next to look for whatever relic was in the warden's office that could help Selena. If he got caught, then I wouldn't have to worry about him. And if he got what we needed, that would be helpful too.

Win-win situation.

"Actually, she does need your help," I told him with a grin.

I loved when things came together.

Selena

"YOU WANT ME DELIVERING FOOD THERE?" I all but whimpered as Boris told me that my duties today would include Seth's section of the prison.

"Do you have a problem with that?" he growled as he spooned a cup of what looked like slop into a few bowls and began to put them on my cart.

"No," I told him reluctantly, scared to make a fuss about anything, thanks to the stolen goods hiding in my room and the rumors that I knew were flying around about me. A bead of sweat slid down my forehead, and the room's temperature seemed to spike.

I smiled at Boris, getting a disgruntled grunt in return, and I began the trek to Seth's cell.

I was nervous.

We'd barely spoken since he'd brought me back from death. With everything that had happened with Alaric and Keon...and I suppose Laz, I was starting to feel guilty about the freeze out after he'd saved me.

But every time my anger started to chill, I would see him with that girl...his fiancée, and all the hurt and anger would come rushing back.

The trip to Seth's section of the prison seemed much quicker today. The guard walking behind me was silent, and I longed for a talkative one to keep me distracted. Granted, those kinds of guards were usually saying disgusting things to me, but at least it would be distracting.

The wails of the prisoners were louder here. You could taste the despair in the air. I passed by a cell where the prisoner was nothing but a pile of rags on the ground. When I set down the tray, the rags didn't move.

Something told me they wouldn't move again.

Butterflies took flight in my stomach as I wheeled the tray up to Seth's cell. I frowned when he wasn't waiting on his cot like he usually was. The guard wasn't really paying attention as he opened the cell door, and Seth was suddenly there with a piece of concrete from the wall, smashing it against the guard's head.

The guard fell to the ground as I choked on a scream. Seth dragged the guard into the cell and threw a blanket over him. I stood there in shock. Seth looked revitalized…better than I'd ever seen him. Was it the crystal? And why had he just done that to the guard? Once the other guards and the warden found out, Seth would be lucky to be left alive.

He was there in front of me then, pulling me into his arms. "You have to let me explain," he whispered hurriedly. "You can't shut me out anymore."

"Seth, what is going on?" I breathed, the weak girl inside of me savoring the feel of his arms after so long without them.

"I'm desperate for you. I thought I could do it, push you away. But I'm weak. You should want nothing to do with me, because my entire kingdom is on the brink of destruction and all I can think about is the last time I felt your lips, the last time I touched you. How did I get to the point where I'm endangering everything just on the off chance that I can see your smile again?"

"Who was she?" I asked, my voice trembling as my heart reminded me of how much it had hurt to see him with her.

"My only connection to Fairie," he told me, touching our foreheads together as his hands moved up and down my arms. "She was my betrothed before everything happened, before my father was killed and I was framed." He brushed a kiss across my lips, cutting off my gasp at his revelation. "She's screwing my cousin but still in love with me. She gives me tidbits about Fairie, things that I hope to use if I ever get out of here."

"Do you love her?" I asked painfully, my heart clenching at the thought. Over the last few weeks, I'd tried to rip him from my heart, but ten seconds in his presence and I realized that I was still totally and desperately in love with the broken, complicated fae in front of me.

"No," he said firmly, and my heart unclenched a bit from the confidence in his answer. "I was a boy when I loved her, I scarcely knew the meaning. And now..."

"And now what?" I asked him, my insides fluttering with hope about what he was about to say.

"And now I know I never knew what love was... until you."

"You love me?" I whispered, because sometimes it

was hard to believe that was possible, that one person, let alone three, could have those kinds of feelings for me. I'd gone my whole life without feeling any kind of love.

And I didn't want to trust it.

But his lips were right there.

"You own me," he whispered. "I'm beginning to think there isn't anything I wouldn't do for you, even if it damned me and everything else in the world to do it."

My breath hitched as he leaned closer to me and then stopped.

"Kiss me," he demanded, but it was more beseeching than it was anything else.

"Seth," I whispered, unsure.

His lips closed over mine then, silencing my fears. His tongue dipped in sweetly, shallowly, teasing me. Melting me. When he pulled away, I felt lightheaded. Just then, it didn't feel like we were in a dark cell, chaos bound to descend at any minute. It didn't feel like most days, where all I felt was hate and hurt from him.

It felt like we were stealing a little bit of peace.

And I wanted that so bad.

He pulled back and looked at me, a silent question in his gaze. I responded by pressing my lips against his once more. My mouth sealed over his, a sweet, slow, desperate dragging of lips. When we finally pulled away from each other, we were both breathing heavily.

"Please," I murmured, weirdly hoping that he hit the guard hard enough that he would be out for a while.

Because this was happening. I felt like I'd been waiting for this moment forever.

"Tell me what you want me to do?" he asked, his voice slightly shaking. "It's been a long time, and this... this means so much more than anything I can remember."

"Kiss me again."

"Is that all?"

I grabbed his head and pulled him to me, losing myself in the taste and scent of him, his skillful kisses unravelling me further. He pulled away and slid his mouth down my neck, licking and sucking until I wriggled against the sensation.

"I've been craving you since the moment I saw you," he murmured.

The craving he spoke about had overwhelmed me too. I had a confusing need for this fae to hold and complete me, even though I'd been fighting this feeling for months.

Giving in to the longing, I winded a hand around his neck, stroking his hair. Seth made a soft noise in his throat and shifted closer. I ran my tongue along his bottom lip, and he responded with a fierce kiss, our teeth almost colliding as our tongues pushed against each other. Our hearts thumped in rhythm, matching the way our lives had somehow collided together.

However much I told myself that this wasn't what I wanted, that anything with the four of them wasn't what I wanted...my heart seemed to have other ideas.

Seth's stubbled face scratched at mine, and I

welcomed the feel of it. I trembled...the heat we were creating made me feel like we were about to explode, shoot off into the stars that I hadn't seen in what felt like forever.

I pulled away and touched my mouth a little in disbelief that this was happening as I met the eyes of the male who had somehow stolen a part of my soul and given me part of his in return.

"You're it for me, Selena," he said softly.

I was distracted by the sensations I felt just then. The way his body felt against mine, his soft breaths mingling with mine. "You're already in my heart and head. I've spent months trying to get rid of you, and you won't leave," I whispered.

His fingers tightened for a moment as a tremor rushed through his body, like he couldn't believe what I was saying.

And I couldn't believe what I was saying either. Maybe the loss of my power had made me defective.

He led me over to his cot and sat down in front of me, and it said a lot for the moment that I didn't care that the guard was tucked under it. Today, I was wearing the hideous prison uniform that was two pieces, and I didn't regret it as he slowly untucked my top from my pants and began to kiss the skin he exposed, lips cool against the heat as I helped him take it all the way off.

The soft touch lit something inside of me. I ran trembling hands along his back, dragging my fingers across the skin on his back. He flinched as I ran across a lash wound that hadn't quite healed yet. I stiffened, reality threatening to ruin the bubble we'd created.

"It's okay," he murmured, brushing a kiss against my stomach once again and ridding my mind of anything but his lips. He gripped my hips, pulling me close. I drowned in him. He stood up and ran his nose along the sensitive spot at the base of my neck, his breathing heavy to match mine. The heat of his mouth burned my skin.

He nipped my shoulder, then planted soft kisses towards the top of my breasts, palming the soft mounds through my faded bra. He made me feel gorgeous, like I was wearing sexy lingerie instead of a prison uniform and faded underthings.

I fumbled with his shirt, my desire making me clumsy as I pulled the shirt upwards. Seth helped, exposing the smooth lines of his chest. I ran my fingers along his chest and my hands across his shoulders, then traced his arms. Even with all the silver lash scars that never fully faded because of his almost daily torture sessions, he was beautiful. Like a dream really.

In a swift movement, Seth unclasped and dispensed with my bra, his tongue teasing my nipple before I had a chance to react. The sudden intensity pooled hot desire between my legs. I moaned and gripped his shoulders, digging my nails into his flesh.

He began to tease me, his arousal strained against his pants and pushing against my thin pants and underwear. With one hand, he untied the drawstring that held the pair of pants up, and my pants slid to my ankles. I quickly stepped out of them and then pushed against him once again, desperate for the friction.

"I've dreamed about touching you like this from the very first day I saw you. Every single minute your mouth was close enough, I obsessed about kissing you."

As if wanting to make up for lost time, he ran his fingers along my back, stroking gently before moving his hands and cupping my breasts. He circled his thumbs around my hard nipples, and I reached for the string on his pants. I undid it with shaking fingers. He shuffled out of his pants. They joined our clothes, which were strewn across the dirty stone floor. His prison issued grey briefs held a barely restrained erection.

He wanted me, that much was obvious. I hungrily dragged my gaze across his smooth chest, taking in the sight of his rock-hard abs and the lines disappearing into his briefs. He was thinner than the others, but for a guy who was starved regularly, he was amazingly fit looking.

Seth didn't stand for long. He pushed me backwards onto the cot, and when his naked chest met mine, he undid me. I arched my back as he slid a hand beneath my bottom, my hardened nipples brushing against him. Seth groaned, his rigid length pressing against my increasingly sensitive sex. He pulled my leg around his waist and nibbled on my lip as I gasped for breath, drowning in the moment.

He suddenly moved down my body until he was kneeling on the floor in front of me, the warmth of his breath against my sex. He pulled my legs towards him, setting them on his shoulders. I was quivering as he pressed his mouth to me, tongue gliding along my wetness and teasing the sensitive bud. I gripped the edge of the cot and struggled to stifle a cry.

"Fuck, you're perfect..." The vibration of his voice against me intensified the engulfing sensation. He slid a finger inside, continuing to explore me with his hot mouth. Licking, sucking, thrusting with his fingers, he brought me to the brink over and over. Then each time he stopped, prolonging things to the point I was ready to scream at him. Weren't we supposed to be hurrying? Although at the moment, I couldn't remember the reason that was.

The blinding orgasm hit, and I swore those stars that I hadn't seen in so long were suddenly dancing in front of my eyes.

I could feel him hungrily taking the sight of me in. "Fuck, you're beautiful, Selena," he growled, then pressed me into the cot. My heart hammered as our mouths met, teeth clashing with the raw intensity of the kiss. Seth took my wrists in one broad hand and held my arms above my head. I made a breathless sound as Seth's rough kisses shifted towards my breasts, before he closed his mouth around my pebbled nipple. He pushed my legs apart with his knee, fingers travelling up my inner thigh until he discovered my wet center. I bucked against him as he slipped a finger inside, moving his mouth back to mine. His tongue thrusted into my mouth, matching the movement of his finger, and I moved against him, pushing myself against the palm of his hand.

For what felt like eternity, I drowned in the sensation of his attention to my body, his expert kisses and touch bringing me to the brink and then letting me go again, over and over, just like before, until I couldn't take the building pressure anymore. I closed my eyes, a scream building inside my chest.

Stroking my damp hair from my face, he kissed my closed eyes. "I can't believe this is happening. I want you so bad."

Seth nudged my legs apart and stroked me again, before pushing against me. I gasped as the tip of him touched my clit, and it was all I could do not to come just from his touch. Seth thrusted into me then, hard, and I almost cried out. He stilled, aware of my tensing, then pulled out so he was barely inside.

"I love you, Selena," he said, "I'll always love you." The emotion was clear in his beautiful crystalline gaze, and I nodded, unable to speak. A tear escaped, and he kissed it away gently, before thrusting back into me hard. This time, I did cry out, overwhelmed by the new connection to Seth, wanting more of him but aware he'd already given me everything he had, body, heart and soul.

He moved slowly at first, eyes still fixed on mine, before increasing the urgency. The pressure built as the movement bumped my clit. He pulled up one of my legs, and I curled it around his hip. I dug my fingernails into his tense shoulders, and he kissed me, the movement of his tongue matching the push of his hips. Everything overwhelmed into a world of sensation as I spiraled upwards towards the edge of those stars once again.

All I could feel was him inside me, over me, consuming me, and I clutched his waist, giving into the supernova explosion of my orgasm.

Lost in Seth's world, I was aware of his hips tensing before he thrusted hard into me one more time, swearing softly as he came. I wound my arms around him, holding his damp body against mine, his rapid heartbeat slowing. Seth covered my face with kisses, and I relaxed back with my eyes closed, at peace for at least a minute.

* * *

A GROAN SOUNDED from under the cot where we were still wrapped around each other.

"What are we going to do?" I asked anxiously.

"I'll take care of him," a voice came from the darkness right outside the cell.

We both jumped when Keon stepped close to the cell.

"Have you been watching this whole time?" I asked indignantly, furious that he would do something like that.

He held up his hands as if to calm me down. "I just got here. Something came over the speakers that the prisoners in the next block hadn't been fed yet, and I volunteered to come since I knew you were on duty today."

I quickly got up and began to put my clothes on, feeling awkward suddenly.

Another groan, and a hand flopped out from under the cot. Keon sighed and stepped into the cell.

"When you say 'take care of it,' what do you mean by that?" I ventured, not sure that I wanted to know the answer.

"No one will find out about this," he answered calmly, not answering the question outright but giving me enough that I knew the fate of the guard.

But I found myself not really caring.

Sometimes when I had thoughts like that, I wondered if I belonged in Nightmare Penitentiary after all.

"I'd better go," I told Seth reluctantly nodding to my cart of now ice-cold food. He stood up, unashamed of his nakedness. He put his arms around me.

"I love you," he said softly. Keon pretended to be interested in the wall while Seth nuzzled my neck, the sexy fae completely different than any time before. Who knew he'd be a cuddler?

"Oh, I need you to take this with you," he told me, throwing on a pair of pants and moving away from the cot. Keon took that opportunity to drag the hazy-eyed guard out from beneath the cot and hauled him over his shoulder with a grunt.

"Thank you," I told him. He gave me a small, sad smile that told me how he really felt about what he'd walked up on, and then he stroked my face with one hand before he left the cell.

Seth returned with the crystal. I looked at him confused. "I know, you went through a lot to get this back to me. And it does make me heal faster. But it will be safer with you. You're the only one that I trust with it."

"Are you sure?" I asked, grasping it in my hands tightly. He was so revitalized right now. I didn't want him to experience his torture sessions without the crystal.

"It would be far worse for me if it got taken again and we started everything over again."

"Okay," I murmured, tucking it into my pants pocket.

Seth pressed a desperate, quick kiss on my lips. We could hear footsteps getting closer.

"See you soon," he told me before I slipped out of the cell and took off with the cart, right as another guard appeared around the corner.

I walked away with a smile I couldn't contain and ignored the flicker of unease in my heart that told me I knew better.

CHAPTER 13

SELENA

I staggered back to my prison cell after morning shift, exhausted. Alaric had spent the night in my room, and we decided that waking me up every couple of hours might stop the ghost from taking me over.

On the bright side, it worked. The bad part was that now I struggled to keep my eyes open, and I could easily lie on the floor now and I'd fall asleep. But that didn't solve my problem, now did it?

The ghost still resided inside me or clung to me... the jury was still out on which, but there was no doubt she wanted me dead. The funny thing was that by looking at her, she didn't look scary, but I guessed when it came to survival, even ghosts would do anything to remain amongst the living.

One idea that kept revolving around my head was doing a séance and attempting to communicate with the spirit to see if there was another way to fix this, instead of having it kidnap me to steal things or toss me into the sewage, or…try and kill me.

Someone rushed past me, their shoulder knocking into mine, and I stumbled backward, my feet tangling. Next thing, my ass hit the ground, and I grimaced. Laughter surrounded me, so I got up and just kept going. I swore I might as well be in high school somedays.

In my prison cell, there was no sign of Keon or Alaric, so I took the chance to go have a long shower to attempt to stay awake, then I'd hunt down another cup of coffee from the mess hall kitchens. Staff were permitted to access the Nescafé, and I'd already had three cups.

Settling down on my bed, I toed off my shoes and yanked off my socks when a small ringing sound came from the end of my bed. I glanced over just as Keon's little mouse hopped up on the mattress. Another small chime came from the rustic looking bell he carried in his mouth. The thing was half his size and resembled the huge church bells, rustic with a small metal ring at one end.

"What have you got there?" I leaned over and picked it up as the mouse made himself comfortable and began chewing on his back leg. The idea of fleas crossed my mind, but I wasn't exactly going to shoo him away when he'd just brought me a gift. Plus after what Keon had told me, I now adored this little guy.

I ran a finger over the outside surface of the bell, where numerous patterns lined the metal, swirls that all looped together. There was no end or start to this. The inside was painted black and the same for the clapper.

"It's very pretty," I said to the mouse and rang it as if calling the dinner bell.

A shiver laced my body, raising all the hair on my arms. In a flash, the British ghost pest tore out of me like a white blur. But just as fast, she zipped back inside, leaving behind the words, "What did you do?" hanging in the air.

I flinched back, clutching the bell in my fist, my thumb inside it to stop it from ringing.

My head buzzed with what just happened, then I jerked my head toward the mouse. "Is this who I think it was?" I whispered, my heart thumping in my chest. "You took this from the warden?"

He squeaked, his little whiskers twitching, and I might not have spoken mouse, but I was one hundred percent certain he'd just said yes.

I wanted to scream with excitement and leapt to my feet, pacing in front of the bed. "Do you know what this means?"

He just looked at me, watching me going back and forth. "It means we can use it to exorcise myself. Oh. My. God. I could kiss you right now."

He made a strange squeaking sound and seemed to physically pull away from me.

"Keep your furry pants on, I'm not going to actually kiss you." Especially if he had fleas. "But you are a magician to have found this and know exactly what I needed. You really can understand me, hey?"

He just stared up at me.

I started pacing again, murmuring to myself. "So clearly, the trinket only works if I'm holding the bell, since nothing happened until I touched it. Good to know. But now, how do I use it? I rang the bell, and she came out of me. Then what?"

"Then what?" a deep male's voice came from the doorway, startling me so much, I shuddered as I spun around, my hand with the bell loosening. Next thing, the bell fell.

My stomach dropped all the way to my feet.

Instinct had me throwing myself after the bell, my knees hitting the ground. I caught it in my palm, the ringing coming once again.

Like before, the ghost yo-yoed out of my body, vanishing inside me like a slingshot, leaving behind her screeching words, "You're making a miisssttaakkkeeee."

Gasping for air, I sat there, my finger inside the bell to stop making any sounds, and then I realized I never should have gone for it as it shouldn't affect me if I wasn't touching it. But I panicked. Crap.

"Are you okay?" I glanced up to Keon, who had me by my arms and lifted me to my feet. "What were you just doing?"

"Did you see her?" I blurted, flopping down on the bed. "The ghost just flung out of me and then back in."

"I didn't see anything." He crouched in front of me,

his hands on my knees and worry crammed behind his gorgeous eyes. "Did you fall asleep?"

"No, your mouse brought me the trinket from the warden's room." I showed him the bell in my grasp, ensuring it didn't make a sound. "And when I ring it, she flings out of me for seconds."

His eyes widened and swept from me to the bell to his mouse.

Keon beamed, and he scooped up his mouse. "Dude, you did this? You are amazing." He kissed it on the head and the critter seemed to almost swoon in his hand.

"He has fleas, and now you are not kissing me with a mouse mouth." Not to mention, the little thing recoiled when I mentioned kissing it. I shook that away. Being rejected by a mouse was not going to bother me.

Setting the mouse back on the bed, Keon turned to me. "Hand it over, so you don't accidently ring the bell."

I nodded, gingerly lifting my fist and placed the item in his palm on its side so as I lifted my finger from the clapper, it remained flush to the side.

Releasing it, I flung my hand back as if I'd just cut the wrong wire on a ticking time bomb.

He closed his fist around the bell and placed it into the pocket of his pants.

"So what now?" I asked.

"How do we use it to eliminate the ghost? What do we know about it so far? It comes out when you're asleep and the trinket can draw her out of you anytime." He glanced over to his mouse and winked. The little critter then scurried away and vanished into a hole in the wall.

"Well, it's not just when I'm asleep actually. I never thought much of it until now, to be honest."

"Selena," he reprimanded me with that deep voice.

"She kinda appeared first in a bathroom I randomly found one day when I was exhausted…and she made a show while we were having sex in the yard."

He stiffened. "She watched us?" He rubbed his chin, almost grinning, and of course that would pique his interest.

"She wasn't there to admire us, but give me tips apparently on having better sex." I huffed. "How would a dusty old British ghost from the 1800s be an expert at sex? You know she called me a prostitute?"

"What sort of tips?" His lips quirked.

I sighed. "Fine, we're not having this conversation now. I have the trinket to help me, so let's stay focused."

His lips pinched. "Of course. You can tell me later. So, she first came to you when you were tired in the bathroom. And each time afterward was the same?"

I nodded. "I think it's when my mind is too weak to fight her that she takes advantage of that moment. So sleep and exhaustion."

"Well, then we need to conduct a ritual that will draw her out, and then we send her back to wherever the hell she came from."

I leaned forward. "And you can do that?"

"Fuck no, but Seth should be able to. He's got magic in his bloodline."

"Okay. I think he'll help us. Oh, reminds me. Was everything all right with that guard in Seth's cell yesterday?" Heat flared up my neck at the memory that Keon knew Seth and I were having sex, yet he covered for us from getting caught.

He nodded quickly. "Yeah, all taken care of. Like I said, nothing you need to worry about anymore."

"What are you both conspiring to?" Alaric barked as he strolled inside, and I almost jumped out of my skin at how focused I was on Keon.

"God, please stop scaring me like that," I said, my heart racing.

He looked at me puzzled. Keon was on his feet and gave Alaric a long-winded rendition of what I'd told him.

"The ghost watched you both have sex?" Alaric grinned, nodding his head as if that was the most important element of what he'd just learned.

I rolled my eyes. "Seriously. We have a solution. Stop thinking with your cocks."

I could physically see their postures straighten as they glanced my way. "Okay, then we do this tonight," Keon said.

"Why not now?" I asked, ready to get this done.

"Because just before lock down of all doors, I can collect Seth without raising the alarms."

"Okay, so we have a plan," Alaric said. "You get Seth, and I'll stay with Selena."

"Then we meet in the small courtyard," I added.

"Deal," Keon said and headed out of my room.

Alaric turned to me, one of his eyebrows arching. "What courtyard?"

* * *

THE FULL MOON hung heavily pregnant in the night sky. It was almost as if the universe had planned for us to have a ritual tonight, putting on a show with no clouds. Grass crunched under my bare feet as I stepped deeper into the yard. I'd read enough to know magic came from the elements, and tonight, we were conducting some kind of ghost exorcism from me, so bare feet it was. It should be pitch dark out here, but with the moon so large, it cast everything in its silvery glow.

Alaric studied the open yard Laz had shared with me. "Why didn't I know about this space?"

I shrugged. "Nightmare Penitentiary holds lots of secrets."

"You sound just like the warden."

"I do not." I shivered at the thought, while my stomach churned with how tonight would go.

I glanced up at the moon, whispering under my breath, "Please let this work."

Alaric suddenly stood behind me, the warmth from his body wrapping over me like a blanket. His arms were belts around my middle, and I leaned back against his hard chest.

"You'll be all right," he reassured me, then kissed the top of my head. "You're not alone in this. Never again alone. I'm never going to let you go from my side ever again."

My mouth curled upward of its own accord, as the promise of his words was something I'd wanted for so long. Just to have family, someone who loved me back. As mismatched as we were, the small group of family I made in prison meant the world to me.

I kissed his forearm. "You don't know how much that means to me."

Just then, a knock came from the door leading back into the building. Alaric marched over and opened it for Keon and Seth to stroll outside, and my heart beamed. But then a fifth person walked out behind them, and I blinked.

"Laz?" I gasped. Was I missing something?

He wore a grin, meeting mine as he kicked the door shut behind him, then locked it with the key sitting in the keyhole. "Apparently, you need my help tonight." The cockiness of his voice made me half laugh.

"Yeah, don't get used to it," Keon barked back.

"What's going on?" I asked as they all approached me. Four powerful men, towering over me, each carrying such heavy baggage from their past, their history lined with darkness. But I clicked with each of them like their darkness fit mine.

"A ritual to send a ghost back requires energies to be drawn from four different beings," Seth explained, reaching over, his hand cupping my chin, lifting my head to face him. I couldn't help but smile looking into his eyes, remembering our bonding last time we were together. "And you are the fifth, Selena. The soul to tie us all together. Once we begin, it will go rather fast. The biggest problem," he said, staring at everyone around us, "is ensuring the ghost doesn't latch itself to one of us. So don't break from the ritual, no matter what you do."

"Got it," Alaric responded. "And what exactly are we doing?"

Seth released me and turned to Keon. "Did you bring the salt?"

Keon pulled out two small sacks of salt from his pockets and handed them over to Seth. We all stepped aside as Seth tore one bag open and proceeded to make a large circle on the side of the lawn where the grass was shorter and there were patches of bare earth.

"So, this is something you guys do regularly?" Laz asked, hands deep in his pockets, slouching on one leg.

"Nope," Alaric answered curtly, and I went over to Laz.

"Did they tell you what we're doing tonight?" It still surprised me that of all the people, they asked Laz. I didn't ask to sound ungrateful, but it did play on the back of my mind that Keon must have known there was more going between Laz and I.

"Yeah, I got the lowdown. You're possessed by a horny ghost who is trying to kill you, and we're getting rid of it tonight."

I cut a glare over to Keon, who chuckled.

"Thanks for helping us." I turned back to Laz. "But in no way is the ghost horny."

"Didn't get much of a choice, but for you, I'd help in a heartbeat." His voice would have definitely reached Alaric and Keon.

I thanked the stars that no one said a word about it. My nerves were jumpy enough without dealing with jealousy.

"We're ready," Seth called out.

My throat suddenly went dry, and I wasn't sure I could get my legs to move. Seth instructed where each guy was to stand around the circle of salt. North, south, east, west, he'd told them, then he glanced over at me, stretching his arm out in my direction.

"Are you ready, beautiful?"

"Yes, I want this over with already."

Quick steps took me to his side where I accepted his hand, and he walked me to the center of the circle, then he took his spot in front of me at the north position.

"At your feet is the bell," he explained, and I looked down to find it nestled in a small cluster of grass. "I am going to begin a chant to bind us all together. No matter what, no one is to break the circle. And when I stop chanting and give you a nod, Selena, pick up the bell and ring it."

"Then what?" I asked.

"Then the ancients from the afterlife will come to collect her back to where she belongs. Like I said, it should go rather quick."

"I'm ready," I said, standing tall and keeping my trembling arms by my sides. I didn't know why I was so nervous. If something bad was going to happen, Seth would have warned us. What was the worst case scenario? It didn't work and we tried again?

Silence fell upon us, and Seth's words played through my head over and over about what I had to do. It wasn't brain surgery, but with how fast my pulse was racing, I wasn't sure I could count two plus two right then without overthinking it.

Seth started to hum, followed by soft words falling from his lips in a language that sounded like a song. I wished I understood what he said. I found myself swaying on the spot. It wasn't long before the atmosphere changed from a cool night to a chill that covered my skin in goosebumps. Seth spoke with power, with eloquent persuasion by his authoritative tone alone. I could easily picture him leading his father's kingdom if he ever cleared his name and got out of here. I intended to do everything in my power to assist him, even if that meant just being there for him. He was a force to be reckoned with. All the men outside with me were.

Electricity suddenly danced in my hair, cracking across my nape. Instantly, a yellow static line flickered outward from Seth, zipping over to Alaric, Laz, and then Keon, before closing up into a perfect circle back with Seth.

I stood in the middle, and no one grimaced or

appeared to be in pain, so whatever that line was, the deterrent wasn't for the living.

At once, Seth fell silent, and over the land came a stillness, a quiet so deafening that it took me a long pause to realize Seth stared at me, then his gaze lowered to the ground.

Right, the bell. Hell! *Get it together, Selena.*

Hastily, I crouched and picked up the bell, then started to ring it, figuring that was the intention. The jingling seemed to echo around us, sharp and peeling through the night.

I held my breath, waiting, expecting. I never stopped shaking the damn bell.

But nothing came.

Not a single beep.

Was it too much to believe the chanting alone got rid of the ghost?

I stared at Seth and shrugged. Did I forget to do something? I glanced around, and everyone looked just as confused. I lowered the bell, left with only silence.

"Why isn't it working?" Alaric asked.

"Maybe you need a bigger bell?" Laz suggested.

"Nah, the chants need to be louder," Keon added.

But I kept my gaze on Seth, searching his face, his eyes. He never so much as twitched but seemed to mumble something under his breath.

Even after a long pause, nothing.

"Why isn't she showing?" I whispered.

He slowly shook his head. "It should have worked."

"Selena, did you tell him the ghost comes out when you are super tired?" Keon said.

"No wonder it's not working, she's so tense, I can see the veins in her temple pulsing," Alaric added.

He could? I couldn't help but reach up to run my fingers over my temple, not feeling any popping veins.

"It's just a figure of speech, babe," he murmured.

"Quiet," Seth bellowed.

My breathing grew more erratic, and suddenly, I felt like this was a waste of my time.

I sighed, then I noticed Seth had his eyes closed, his voice changing as he began chanting a less beautiful song, but one with rugged, harsh words. His demeanor changed, brow furrowed, shoulders stiff, lips curled back.

A heartbeat later, the ghost jolted out of me so fast, you'd think she touched an electrical wire.

Alaric's eyes grew wide, and Keon made a gasping sound. They saw her…they finally saw her as well.

She floated, having no legs, her long dress fluttering as she frantically zipped within the circle. Back and forth. Upward. In every direction, she hit the barrier Seth had created.

Suddenly, I wasn't feeling so safe being in here with her. My feet carried me.

"Don't be afraid of her," Laz said from behind me. "You hold the power, not her."

And just as he said that, she swung toward me, her face contorting to look more like a demon than a woman. Black eyes, skin wrinkly, she hissed at me. "What have you done? You will pay for this."

"Fuck you," I threw back.

"Keep ringing the bell," Seth called out.

I did as he instructed, loud and constant.

She started trembling, shaking harder and harder, like she'd explode any moment now. Before I could even react, she flung herself at me.

She came so fast, I didn't have time to duck.

Claws slashed at my face, tearing skin across my cheek. I shoved against her, wincing from the stinging pain. But she kept lashing out like a psycho.

The men screamed things I couldn't make out. So I did everything I could to survive. I dumped the bell and started punching her back. Apparently in this circle, she took corporal form, my hits not sinking through her, but colliding into her face, her chest, her stomach.

I gave everything I had, driving her back. In a whirlwind, she spun on the spot so violently, it took me off guard. And when she charged at me that way, she collided into my chest so hard, I was thrown off my feet and collided into the wall, right next to Alaric.

He roared with fury, his face red, but my ears were ringing, my heartbeat too loud.

And she was coming for me again.

I scrambled to my feet and ducked her swinging clawed hand that time, but she turned on me too fast for me to escape.

Nails raked down my back. I screamed and hit the

ground. But I'd never give up and rolled onto my back and kicked her right in the knees, giving me a moment's pause to scramble to my feet to see Alaric trembling with anger. Laz bellowed, and Keon was half transformed into his demon form. Fuck, he was going to lose it.

Seth snarled words that made no sense, when his gaze fell onto Keon, fear blanching his face.

I rushed to Seth. "You need to stop this now. Stop before Keon changes." I banged on the invisible wall just as a locomotive slammed into my back. I cried out and crumbled to the ground.

Seconds was all it took.

The invisible wall disintegrated and the men's voices were suddenly suffocating me. They ran toward me, helping me up. Seth was at Keon's side, placing a palm to his brow to calm his beast.

But no matter how much I hurt, how much I cried with agony, I shoved to stand up, pushing past Alaric and Laz to see the ghost back in her transparent form.

She ran for the door.

"Stop her," I called out, everyone turned in the direction I pointed, as she glanced back over her shoulder at us, smiling, glowing eyes and razor-sharp teeth exposed.

"You'll pay for this," she screeched and threw herself right through the door, vanishing inside the penitentiary.

I madly rushed after her, Laz and Alaric behind me. I caught the ends of her dress as she turned a corner.

Desperately, we chased her. Coming around the corner, she was nowhere in sight. At least a dozen beefy men stood in our way, laughing, barking, talking. Hard to tell, but I saw no sign of her. Alaric grabbed my arm and wrenched me backward, Laz stepping in front of us as one of the inmates looked our way. Laz greeted them, apologizing for interrupting them, while Alaric dragged me back outside.

"Stop, what are you doing? She's gotten away. God, maybe she entered one of those prisoners."

Laz joined us seconds later, then shut the door. "Fuck, that was close."

"Why did we stop? Seth said we're sending her back. I don't want her loose in the prison."

"Listen, babe," Alaric said, grasping my shoulders, forcing me to face him. "There are some really bad people in this place. Some that don't even come out until after dark. Even the guards are scared of them. And those are the scariest sonsofbitches you'll ever meet. Fuck the ghost. We got it out of you, that's what matters to me."

My stomach twisted on itself. "Who the hell are those men?" They looked like ordinary prisoners to me.

Keon and Seth approached us as well, and I looked up at Keon, who smiled and looked like his normal self. Then he said, "Alaric is right. They are a cult, a pack of shifters and deathly loyal to Perseus. He's a rare shifter who transforms into four animals, each predatory, and one is the kraken. When it comes out, blood runs down the prison walls for days. If the ghost took one of them as her next host, let them have her. This is no longer our business."

"You're free," Seth said, taking my hand and pulling me toward him. "This is a win, and we need to celebrate. A spirit like her can only spend seconds in this realm without a connection with a host. She's not coming back to haunt you, that's impossible."

Then why didn't I feel safe?

Everyone around me hugged and kissed me, while my heart refused to slow down. Was it really a win?

The ghost was out of me. She might have gone to haunt some other sucker, but she was still in the prison with us. And her words refused to leave my head.

You'll pay for this.

CHAPTER 14

SELENA

It was strange how light I felt after getting rid of the spirit. I hadn't quite realized just how much it had been pulling me down. Without it sucking on my soul, I saw the world in different colors. Things felt more settled, more positive. It no longer felt like I was living in a world of absolutes where I'd never get my power back, where I'd never be able to trust the four…yes, four men that I was falling in love with.

I sat down in the cafeteria, Laz falling closely behind. He squeezed my knee as we settled in. I hungrily picked up the sandwich from my tray and started to dig in.

"Good to see a smile on your face again, sweetheart," he murmured, and I blushed at the way he was looking at me.

Maybe it was possible for me to be happy. Maybe these four men were the universe's penance for all the shit it had dragged me through.

I really needed to find some wood to knock on after thinking something good like that.

Laz kept me laughing and smiling throughout lunch. He had a dry sense of humor that always kept me guessing, and I found myself laughing more than I had in maybe forever throughout the meal.

I was smiling the entire walk back to my cell, and it took me a second to realize that my cell door shouldn't have been wide open. I'd definitely closed it before leaving this morning. I hurried inside, freaking out about the crystal. I couldn't carry it around with me, just in case one of the resident pickpockets targeted me, so I'd hidden it behind a loose stone I'd found in the wall under my cot.

Crouching down and reaching for the rock that held my hiding place, I breathed a sigh of relief when I saw that the crystal was still there. I didn't have anything else in my cell of value to worry about besides this. But this was a very big thing to worry about.

I squinted my eyes when it seemed that the crystal was glowing more than usual. I reached out and grabbed it. As soon as the smooth stone touched my skin, everything around me went black.

I found myself in a beautiful room, the walls made up of glimmering marble, and the floors were an obsidian black. A man wearing a frosted crown stood in front of me, and he looked vaguely familiar. I realized why he looked so familiar when Seth strolled in. A healthy, vibrant looking Seth who took my breath away. He had a shine to him like sunlight was following him with every step he took. I noticed he had what looked like a golden wand attached to a belt around his waist.

"Father," he said respectfully, bowing his head slightly. The king smiled and touched two fingers to his son's cheek. "My son."

The scene changed just then. The king was standing at a window, a pensive look on his face. I watched as a fae with long ebony hair and face that held some of the same features as the king and Seth approached him from behind. The king didn't make a move to show that he'd heard him. The fae held up what looked like Seth's golden wand above his head. The king finally heard him and had just turned his head when the fae's hands came down, stabbing the king right in his chest.

I gasped watching it, my pulse beating rapidly as the king looked at the male in shock and then sunk to his knees, pulling at the weapon lodged in his chest. He finally collapsed to the ground, his eyes rolling back in his head.

Only then did I notice that the fae was wearing a pair of gloves.

I came awake with a start, swaying slightly as the room came back into focus.

Seth. I needed to tell him what I saw. But who was the male that I saw?

I stood up, covering the crystal, still swaying slightly and went to leave my cell. But just as I did, a guard appeared in the doorway. Unease sliced across my chest. "The warden wants to see you now!" he barked.

Panicked at what he'd want now, I followed the guard out of my cell.

Keon was waiting outside of the warden's office, a grim look on his face.

"What's this about?" I whispered to him, but before Keon could answer, the guard ushered me inside the office.

The warden was sitting at his desk. When he heard me, he lifted his head and stared at me for a long moment, something that looked a little bit like regret in his gaze.

He blinked and the look was gone, probably nothing but my imagination.

"You'll be escorted out of the prison today for a leave day," he announced.

"What?" I asked, flabbergasted.

He cleared his throat. "Your mother is dead. Julian murdered her after what happened the other day. Her funeral is being held this afternoon." There was a pause, and I could almost hear the apology in that silence.

The warden cleared his throat again as my knees buckled under me and I began to collapse, only held up when a pair of arms that I recognized as Keon's caught me just in time.

"Keon will be escorting you to the funeral and you'll have a tracker on you, so don't get any ideas."

I couldn't say anything because my mind was having trouble processing what he'd just said. I finally looked up at the warden.

"My mother's dead?" I asked softly, feeling like this was all a dream, some kind of weird aftereffect after we'd exiled the ghost.

The warden's momentary sympathy was obviously gone, replaced by frustration with my inability to pull myself together.

"You need to get going if you don't want to miss the funeral. Give my regards to Julian," he said before turning his back and signaling the conversation was over.

Give my regards to...

Bastard. Of course there would be no repercussions to Julian.

That was just for the rest of us.

I lunged towards the warden, but Keon's arms prevented me from getting anywhere. He dragged me out of the office kicking and screaming. Once away from the warden, I began to sob against Keon, clenching his shirt tightly.

I hated her, but I'd also loved her. I wasn't sure what exactly I was mourning. Maybe it was simply the fact that I would never have a chance for her to love me.

Keon's footsteps stopped. I lifted my head and saw that we'd made it to the front entrance of the prison, something I hadn't seen since that first day.

The enormous doors slowly swung open. And the sun was there, not concealed by clouds, its light almost blinding me after months and months of nothing but shadows and darkness.

Keon set me down, and I took my first steps out of the prison.

It was a strange thing, but the sunlight in that moment felt alien and unfamiliar. I felt like a stranger under the clear, blue sky. The sounds of birds flying above me screeched against my ears.

I realized something terrifying just then—the sunlight no longer felt like home.

Nightmare Penitentiary had changed me. I'd become a part of its darkness. And somehow, it felt sweeter than the sun.

What had I become?

To Be Continued...

Get Book 4, Siren Redeemed here

SWEET DESTINY

BOOK 4

One man broke me. One led me to sin. And one killed me to save me.

I grew up under the iron fist of a vampire. And when I betrayed him, I ended up in Nightmare Penitentiary.

Multiple attacks, my death, and four psycho men later…I'm done being everyone's target.

I have to escape the monsters who surround me within these

walls. So a deal has been struck, and failure to fulfill my part of the bargain is not an option.

With my fae prince, incubus, hellhound, and serial killer, I'm set to unleash hell on all of who've done me wrong.

I've had enough of the cages that surround me.

Sometimes all you need is a second chance to make things right. But in my case, I was given four...

ACKNOWLEDGMENTS

We're so grateful for the enthusiasm you all have had for this series! We love Selena and her band of merry psychos! A special thanks to Summer for being the best beta anyone could ask for. Another thanks to Caitlin and Sarah who keep us running smoothly and are always there with support when we need it!

And to our readers…we love you so freaking much!

C.R. JANE

A Texas girl living in Utah now, I'm a wife, mother, lawyer, and now author. My stories have been floating around in my head for years, and it has been a relief to finally get them down on paper. I'm a huge Dallas Cowboys fan and I primarily listen to Beyonce and Taylor Swift...don't lie and say you don't too.

My love of reading started probably when I was three and with a faster than normal ability to read, I've devoured hundreds of thousands of books in my life. It only made sense that I would start to create my own worlds since I was always getting lost in others'.

I like heroines who have to grow in order to become badasses, happy endings, and swoon-worthy, devoted, (and hot) male characters. If this sounds like you, I'm pretty sure we'll be friends.

I'm so glad to have you on my team...check out the links below for ways to hang out with me and more of my books you can read!

**Join my Facebook readers' group:
www.facebook.com/groups/C.R.FatedRealm/**

Visit my website: www.crjanebooks.com/

Bestselling author, Mila Young tackles everything with the zeal and bravado of the fairytale heroes she grew up reading about. She slays monsters, real and imaginary, like there's no tomorrow. By day she rocks a keyboard as a marketing extraordinaire. At night she battles with her mighty pen-sword, creating fairytale retellings, and sexy ever after tales. In her spare time, she loves pretending she's a mighty warrior, walks on the beach with her dogs, cuddling up with her cats, and devouring every fantasy tale she can get her pinkies on.

Join my Facebook reader group.
www.facebook.com/groups/milayoungwicke-
dreaders

www.ingramcontent.com/pod-product-compliance
Lightning Source LLC
Chambersburg PA
CBHW020802190726
48285CB00006B/2142